FROM

MASOR + LADY MARY BOSCAWEN.

CHRISTMAS 1967.

JILL TRIES OUT HER FAVOURITE

Page 99

Jill
and Prince the Pony

JOAN DICKINS

Illustrated by Stanley Lloyd

BLACKIE: LONDON AND GLASGOW

Also by Joan Dickins:

JILL AND PRINCE TRIUMPH AGAIN

BLACKIE & SON LIMITED
5 FITZHARDINGE STREET
PORTMAN SQUARE
LONDON . W.I

BISHOPBRIGGS, GLASGOW

BLACKIE & SON
(INDIA) LIMITED
103-5 FORT STREET
BOMBAY

PRINTED IN GREAT BRITAIN BY S.C.W.S. LTD. (PRINTING DEPT.), GLASGOW, S.W.I

CONTENTS

ILLUSTRATIONS

CHAPTER I

Letters

" Oh, gosh!" said Jill, flopping down on her bed, a letter in her hand.

" What is it?" asked a head thrust out through the curtains of the next cubicle. It was Janet Mettleton, Jill's best friend.

" I've got to stay with Aunt Mary for a month." Jill shook back her brown plaits and looked up at Janet, indicating the letter.

" Who's she?" Janet appeared in pyjama trousers and vest, and perched on Jill's bed, which was littered with clothes and papers.

" She's a beastly old thing. Terribly prim and proper. You have to sit indoors and read encyclopedias or sew all day."

" Not really?"

" Well—not quite so bad, I suppose. She took me to the Zoo last year. Mum and Dad have been invited on a yachting party, and Mum says I can't go, because it'll be all grown-ups and boring." Jill's pleasant expression changed to one of disgust.

" I expect it will be," said Janet. " Can't you go to

some other relative? I wish I could have you, but we're going to France."

"Thanks awfully, Janet, I know you can't. The trouble is, Aunt Mary likes me," said Jill, smiling ruefully.

"Can't you smash the best tea-set, or frighten the cat into fits?" Janet expected other people to be as crazy as she was.

Jill laughed and shrugged her shoulders, then went on dressing.

"Oh, well, I shall just have to stick it," she said.

"Anyway, thank heavens we break up to-morrow," said Janet. "What train are you catching?"

"The 10.37," said Jill. "Are you going straight to Dover?"

"Yes, the parents are picking me up there. Oh, hullo, Betty!" she called as a tall, fair-haired girl passed.

"Hullo!" Betty stopped and grinned. "I'm going to North Wales," she said. "Isn't it super? We've changed our plans."

"Lucky beggar!" sighed Jill.

"What's up?" asked Betty.

"I'm staying in London," said Jill, "with a ghastly great-aunt."

"Ha, ha!" said a short, freckled girl as she passed. This was Nancy, Jill's greatest enemy. "*I'm* going to Cornwall. Ya! Poor little girlie, who's staying in London!"

Jill sprang up and laid about the teaser with a pillow. Nancy dashed to a wash-basin and threw a glass of water over Jill.

Unfortunately Matron came in just then, and surveyed the wet, feathery mess and panting opponents.

"Who did this?" she asked quietly. "I see I need not ask." Jill dropped the sadly flattened pillow, and her enemy

A GLASS OF WATER FOR JILL

put down the glass. "Report to me after you have cleared up this." Her voice rose on the last word, and her hand hovered vaguely over the floor. "In fact, you had better report yourselves to Miss Carslake after breakfast."

She swept out of the room.

"You started it!" said the unabashed Nancy, blushing hotly.

"Oh no, she didn't," said Janet, "you—you *indited* her!"

"Incited, you mean." Dorothy came over and sneered at them, then returned to the window, where she continued to contemplate the view.

"How does Dorothy sneer like that?" whispered Janet. They all screwed up their faces and pulled their lips about, in an effort to imitate that wonderful twitch of superiority which Dorothy had; and then they nearly died laughing at each other's faces.

. . . .

Mr. and Mrs. Hever were sitting at breakfast, when Mrs. Hever suddenly said,

"Oh, Bill, Marjorie's written again. Do you want to hear it?"

"Yes, if you like, dear. Does she say anything of particular interest? If so, skip the rest."

"All right, dear. Well—

"Dear Ann,

How are you and your fine family? Mine is fit, but grumbles too much. I thought——"

Just then Pat Hever came clattering down the stairs, and burst in.

"'Morning, Mum. 'Morning, Dad." She sat down, and shook her dark, short hair back.

" Pat, why are you late?" Father's and daughter's grey eyes met and held.

" Sorry, Dad. I was looking at that stamp catalogue you gave me the other day. Do you know, those Cubans are worth a shilling each."

" Oh, all right." He smiled, and his eyes turned blue. " I suppose I shouldn't get you these things if I want to have you down in time for meals. Yes, dear?" he added, turning to his wife.

" She goes on about the house then." Mrs. Hever stopped and looked through the first page. " Oh, she says she wanted to invite us up this summer, but John had made other plans. They're going on a cruise, the lucky things. Why, they're not taking Jill! She's got to stay in London with a great-aunt."

" Gosh, I bet that's foul," said Pat, swallowing boiled egg too quickly.

" She may like London," said Mr. Hever lightly, his eyes twinkling.

" Oh, Bill! The poor child! How could she? Couldn't we have her down here?"

" But, Mum, Peter and Jane and John are coming! She'd ruin the holiday." Pat began to pout.

" How do you know?" asked her mother mysteriously, brown eyes smiling.

" Oh, well, she might not, of course. But she sounds as if she would. London!"

" Her father's a jolly good sport, and her mother was great fun before she married. She's had a lot of anxiety, with her husband away from home, you know. He was often reported missing. He's a geologist, and travels all over the world. Jill's your own age, and is probably great fun, really." Pat began to relent at these words.

"Gosh! but what shall we do with her? She can have Freddy to ride, if she likes," Pat conceded.

" Well, she can join in your games, if she wants to. You must show her Dartmoor. You can all go swimming, with a picnic—the usual things."

. . . .

" Sugar, Jill?"

" Yes, please, Mum!"

" Well," said Mr. Crewe as he folded up a thick sheet of paper, " your report is quite reasonable, on the whole a great improvement, but what's all this about bad conduct?"

" What!" Mrs. Crewe looked up quickly.

" Well, Nancy and I were fighting. I threw a pillow at her and she chucked some water at me. Then Matron came in."

" Oh, Jill! Why were you fighting?" Mr. Crewe was grinning while his wife spoke. He remembered similar situations in his own school days.

" Oh!" said Jill, and stopped. " I was saying something about having to go to Aunt Mary's, when she remarked that I was a ' poor little girlie '." Jill frowned and looked down. Her father stopped laughing and his liquid hazel eyes turned thoughtfully serious.

A ring at the door broke the sudden silence, and Jill leapt up to see what it was. She came back with a handful of letters. There were two for her mother, three for Mr. Crewe, and a card from Janet, who was in France by now. She said she would write later, when she had more news, which Jill really wanted now.

" John," said Mrs. Crewe, " Ann's written to ask Jill down for the holidays. Do you think she could go?" Jill pricked up her ears.

" Why not? Where does she live? I've forgotten."

(G 391)

" Dartmoor. It's terribly out of the way. No shops or anything for miles."

" Oh, how lovely!" exclaimed Jill.

" Would you really like it, dear? She's very erratic and unusual."

" Oh, Mum, I'd love it. Has she got any children?" Jill sat on the edge of her chair.

" Yes, one girl your age. I believe she has the three children of her friends in India staying there too."

" Jill," said her father suddenly, " how would you like a pony?" He looked thoughtful, and spoke seriously.

" Dad! Do you mean it?" Jill rushed to him, blue eyes afire, and brown plaits flying over her shoulders.

" John, do you think she's safe yet?" Mrs. Crewe looked anxiously at Jill.

" How many lessons have you had, Jill?" asked her father, sitting her on the arm of his chair.

" Fifty-three. I counted them exactly. I've ridden five different ponies too."

" I should say you could manage a quietish pony now, then." He winked at Jill secretly; and Mrs. Crewe agreed to asking Mrs. Hever to find a good Dartmoor pony for their daughter to ride.

.   .   .   .

" Jill," called her mother, a few days later, " will you fetch the two medium-sized suitcases? We'd better pack your clothes to-day."

" All right, Mum."

There was a sound of feet on long-suffering stair carpets, and a good many thumps and crashes, more tramping again, and Jill rushed into the sitting-room, with a suitcase rocking in each hand.

" Oh, Jill, you really mustn't. What the neighbours—

Look out! Oh, you've knocked over that lovely vase Jenny gave me."

" Okay, I've caught it."   Mr. Crewe leant forward quickly and grabbed the blue glass vase before it reached the floor, with the laughter bubbling inside him.

" Jill," he went on, " if that's going to be your style for the next two months, you'd better stay at home."   His daughter turned more quietly.

" Sorry, Dad," said Jill meekly.

" Better at Ann's than at Aunt Mary's, anyway," said her mother.   " Ann's quite wild herself, still," she laughed.

" But all the same, behave reasonably, my infant."   Her father foresaw complications if this was not made clear.

They packed in everything, but with difficulty.   Vests, knickers and blouses were easy, but jodhpurs and skirts were rather unwieldy.

" Do you want your shorts with you, dear? I expect the others will wear them. Here's your bathing costume. That can go in down the sides."   Jill crushed it in.

" Jill had better go to bed now," said Mr. Crewe, " or she'll never get up in time for the ten o'clock train."

" All right. 'Night, Daddy; 'night, Mum."   She kissed her parents and ran up to her room, a little more quietly.   There, she sat at the window, and thought how glad she was to leave London.

.   .   .   .

Jill stood on the platform at Exeter, and looked round for a disengaged porter. The clatter and bustle of the station whirled round her, and she made her way to a seat by the wall. A raucous voice made itself heard above the din, and Jill picked out some phrases.

"—for the Okehampton train go to—three—calling at

—ton, Tiff— and Okehampton change at—hampton for—
Moor Halt and —ly."

Jill caught only a few words, the rest were swallowed up
in the blare of the megaphone's echoes.

" Oh, porter!" she said, holding up her hand. " Could
you please tell me which train I catch for Maddaford Moor
Halt?" The porter bustled over to the young girl.

" Why, yes, missie. We've got five minutes to catch it.
Come along and I'll take yer bags to it, now. We'll 'ave
to 'urry, m'dear."

He picked up Jill's cases and hurried off up the platform. Jill stumbled after him, brushing people as she passed,
getting knocked by their cases, then running up the stairs
to the bridge, and at last finding the porter waiting by an
empty carriage. The train looked very small compared to
the fine express Jill had come down in. She got in and sat
down with a sigh of relief.

" Thank you very much," said Jill, nervously slipping
the porter half a crown, because she had a feeling suddenly
that she ought to. " Do I have to change?"

" No, missie, 'tis a slow train, stopping at most stations.
Thank you, m'dear! Be you on holiday, then?"

Porters love to be polite, especially when they should be
doing some other work.

" Yes," said Jill. " I've never been to Dartmoor before."
She began to feel even more excited.

" Yu'll be sure to like it, then. Be you goin' to ride while
you're there? 'Tis fair good country for that, if you've a
mind to." The porter glanced up the platform, and then
looked back again. Jill liked him, and grinned.

" Oh, I hope so," she said. " Do you ride?" Her eyes
were sparkling as she thought that it would not be long,
although she felt a little nervous.

" Well, I used to, like."

Just then the train began to move, so the friendly porter slammed the door shut and stood back, grinning. Jill waved for a little, and then sat back, letting her mind wander over the possibilities of her visit.

The train rumbled over the Exe, and Jill hung out of the window. Two boys in a rowing dinghy looked up and waved. Jill waved back. She had tried to read on the way down, but the train was so crowded that she couldn't concentrate. Now she felt too excited, and preferred to look out of the window. Soon the train plunged between two crests of the moors. The gradient was steeper, and the train chugged more slowly.

The steep green slopes of a tor rose above them, the distance not apparent because there were no trees or houses.

" Isn't it lovely!" said Jill to herself. " I've never seen anything like it." She leaned out of the window eagerly.

On each side she could see more folds, the tops rough and strewn with great granite boulders, the sides deceptively smooth and graceful. Bracken grew profusely as did the heather, but the latter was not yet in flower.

The train was climbing steadily, and soon Jill could feel the difference in the air, the marvellous cool clearness of it, and the warmth that came from the turf, the rocks, and the heather.

Jill hardly noticed when the train stopped at stations, but at Okehampton a cheery, rosy-faced farmer's wife climbed in, and seeing Jill's newness to Dartmoor, pointed out the better-known tors and ranges.

Soon the train drew to a slow, shuddering stop, and heaved a slow, smoky sigh.

" Here we are!" thought Jill, whose stomach ached a little with nervousness.

CHAPTER II

New Surroundings

Mrs. Hever stood up and looked at her watch.

" I'd better go now, Pat. Will you clear lunch, please?"

" What time does her train get in?" asked John.

" About 3 o'clock, I think. It's 2.15 now, so I think I'd better get ready." Mrs. Hever went out of the room.

" I say," said Jane, " let's go up to where the wood meets the road, and watch as they go past. Then we can see what she looks like."

" Jolly good idea," said Peter. " They'll be along there about 3.30."

Pat and Jane piled the plates and took them into the kitchen.

Peter and John wandered out into the stable yard, and leaned on the paddock fence.

" What do *you* think she'll be like?" John appealed to his elder brother, turning his eyes in the other's direction.

" Oh—I don't know. She may be awful, but you never know. I shall keep an open mind."

" I think she's fat, with pig-tails, and waddles."

Peter laughed, but knew in his heart what he wanted her to be like. She ought to be brown-haired and blue-eyed, well built, but quite tall. She should love horses, and indeed all animals. She must like swimming and running.

" Not a hope," thought Peter. " She's probably dresses terribly neatly, eats very little, and always says the right things."

He turned round and contemplated the house with calm grey eyes. He liked originality.

"It's lovely here," he thought. "The country is beautiful, the air is healthy, and the moors are grand for riding." He sighed and turned back to the fence.

Pat and Jane rushed up.

"Let's go for a ride first, and then get to our vantage point," said Pat, her rather pale face glowing in the sunlight.

She leapt on top of the fence, and seesawed on her stomach.

"Have you got your watch working again?" inquired Jane.

"Just about," Peter replied.

Five minutes later they mounted their ponies and trotted out of the yard. They followed the road the car had taken, and turned into a field. Bracken, Peter's bay pony, burst into a gallop, fighting for his head, and they all four raced over the grass. Peter headed for a low, broken-down place in the hedge, and leapt it nimbly. The girls followed, but poor little Bess, a small brown mare which John rode, trailed her forelegs through some creeper, and landed stumbling. John managed to keep his seat, and soon cantered after the others. They emerged on to a heathy expanse, and taking a likely-looking track, fibrous and dusty, they disappeared from sight.

.   .   .   .

Jill stepped out of the carriage and found herself confronted by a brown-eyed, golden-haired woman in her thirties, who said, "Hullo, you must be Jill Crewe. I'm Mrs. Hever."

"Oh, hullo." Jill smiled, liking her hostess.

PETER TAKES THE HEDGE

" Did you have a reasonable journey, Jill?" Mrs. Hever took a suitcase.

" Oh yes, it was better after Exeter. The moors are lovely!"

" You haven't seen them before?"

" No. It's awfully good of you to invite me down. I shall enjoy myself." Jill remembered her parents' advice.

" Oh, that's all right, Jill. It'll be company for Pat and her friends. Well, we'd better get along home. I expect you feel like some tea by now, don't you?"

" Well, I do feel rather thirsty," admitted Jill.

They went out of the station, and Jill put her cases in the back of the car. They drove off at a terrific rate, but soon had to slow down, for the road was more crowded, much to the mercurial Mrs. Hever's annoyance.

Mrs. Hever and Jill chatted for a little while about school and the weather, and Jill found it easy to talk with such an interesting person.

" Do you like riding?" asked Mrs. Hever. " My hooligans are mad on it."

" Oh yes," said Jill, " I love it."

" That's good. You can ride Freddy, Pat's second pony. He's not much to look at, but he can jump, and he's very handy. Pat's got a new three-year-old pony this year, which she's trying to train. He's quiet enough to hack about, but he hates Horse Shows, because of the crowds. He jumps quite well."

" Freddy sounds lovely," said Jill, leaning forward a little, and imagining that she was already riding him. They drove along in silence for a while, content with their thoughts, and Jill with the new country as well.

The road went steeply up and down hill, then followed a valley. After that, it climbed above the trees and wound over a ridge. Coming down the other side of this, with the wind in their faces, Mrs. Hever pointed out a lovely old timbered house. It had a well-thatched roof, and was mellowed with the weather.

" That's our house," she said proudly, indicating it with a quick wave of the hand.

Jill peered out of the window, and saw it at once. All nervousness had left her.

" Oh, isn't it beautiful!" she breathed. " The surroundings are so green and peaceful."

A little trickle of water ran through the valley where the house lay, and there were numerous trees on the lower slopes.

Hidden amongst those trees, unknown to the two in the car, the other children were discussing Jill, to her disadvantage. They felt that she was " towny " and horribly neat and prim, because she was wearing a suit and, worst of all, a hat.

" She ought to have ringlets, 'stead of plaits," John was saying.

" Come on," said Peter, " we'd better go and meet her. Say ' How do you do ' nicely, John, and make sure your face is clean." He still hoped that Jill would be nice, although he joked with the others.

They all laughed, and broke into a canter along the soft track, which was padded with years of autumn leaves.

Mrs. Hever stopped the car in front of the house, and Jill got out, stretching and yawning after so many hours' travelling.

" Would you like to see your room first, Jill, or just sit down a bit?" Mrs. Hever took the cases out, and then backed the car into a barn opposite the house, while Jill held back the door.

"Well, I'd like to change into something cooler first, please," said Jill; "these clothes are so hot."

She was wearing a suit of quite heavy material, and carrying a full-length coat. Her mother had insisted on these, and they were too heavy to go in the cases.

"Yes, I should, dear. I'll get some lemonade ready while you change." Mrs. Hever's brown eyes smiled.

She led the way into the house, up the stairs leading from a cosy hall on to a wide landing, and into a smallish room facing east and south. It was a pretty room, with flowered chintz curtains and a bedspread of the same stuff. There was a low table and an easy chair, the bed and a dressing-table, and very little else, which gave the room a simple, comfortable feel.

Jill changed into a skirt and blouse, not wanting to wear shorts too soon, as they seemed rather informal. When she got down, Pat and Peter were in the kitchen. Mrs. Hever called her in, and introduced the children.

"Hullo," said Peter, seeing that she looked as he had hoped, and rather surprised.

"I'm glad it's good weather for you," said Pat, grinning, and looking under her eyebrows. Jill grinned back rather hesitatingly.

"Here's the lemonade," said Mrs. Hever, breaking the awkward pause. She put a jug of lemonade on the table, and Pat seized it with joy. Peter grabbed some glasses and rolled them over to Pat. She filled one and handed it to Jill, who accepted it with rather brief thanks.

"Mum?" Pat asked, her voice lifting on the word.

"Yes, please, dear."

She filled three more.

"What about Jane and John?" Mrs. Hever asked, and went to the door, calling them. They rushed in and yelled for lemonade. Jane said hullo to Jill, and smiled. John muttered a greeting, and sat on the table, drinking, his eyes fixed upon her. She drank round the ice cubes, carefully avoiding them, and John giggled. He scrunched up a cube and grinned at Pat. Jill looked at all four children and considered them. She liked Peter, and Jane seemed nice, but she felt Pat's and John's hostility.

Jill finished her drink, and waggled the glass so that she got both bits of ice into her mouth. She sucked them and grinned at John. She felt heartened by this. After the introductions, Peter rocked off the table and said:

" Come and see the ponies now?"

Jill nodded, and the five children raced into the yard. Mrs. Hever looked after them and frowned. She felt that Jill was not liked.

" I must see that she's happy," she thought. " The children mustn't spoil her holiday." Her eyes darkened thoughtfully.

The five in question ran round the side of the house and behind the barn-garage. There the stables appeared, on three sides of an open yard. Mr. Hever was standing at the water-tank, giving a big bay horse a drink.

" There's Daddy and Ben," said Pat. " He's been exercising. Hunting starts next month, or rather, cubbing." Jill looked at Pat and wanted to ask more.

" Hullo, is this Jill?" The tall man stepped forward and offered his hand to Jill. He had a quiet, deep voice, and a calm bearing. Jill saw that the horse loved him, and she realized that he was a person to be respected.

" The other horses are all out," he said. " Would one of you take Ben down to the Long Field for me?"

" Okay," said Peter. " John, I'll give you a leg-up.

You must learn to ride big horses if you're to be a jockey."
Jill's and Peter's eyes met.

John, at ten years old, knew exactly what he wanted to
be. And that was a jockey. He was short, and very light,
though he could not be described as thin. He drew his
knees up on Ben's withers, and leant forward.

Jill looked at John with envy. She loved to hear about
racing, and would have liked to be a jockey, if she had been
a boy. John seemed so composed and sure of his future.

Pat saw Jill's look, but thought it was astonishment.

They went down towards the stream, and took a track,
full of nettles and long grass, which led between two fields.
Jill looked at Jane and grinned as they looked at each other.

" Ow !" said Jill as a nettle stung her leg. Pat was stung
too, but kept quiet just to make Jill look silly. She felt
annoyed: their holiday was ruined.

JOHN KNOWS WHAT HE'S DOING

" Here we are," said John. Peter opened the gate, and Ben cantered through. John sat firm, but suddenly started to slip. In his efforts to get upright, he slid over the other side, and didn't stop till he reached the ground.

The other four laughed, and caught Ben as he started to wander off. John gave him a piece of apple, and took off the bridle. Ben started to graze, and wandered slowly down to the water.

" There are the other horses," said Peter. " The grey is Dorides, the chestnut is Firefly, and the brown is Sandra."

" I like Sandra, he looks intelligent," said Jill, " and Dorides is super." She turned and noticed that Peter's dark hair was curly.

" Sandra's a mare, silly," said John. " Don't you know the difference?"

" Oh yes, sorry. She was behind Firefly. I couldn't really see her." Jill felt squashed.

" The Arabs must be in the next field," said Jane. " We'd better not go so far now, it's nearly tea-time. We can see the ponies on the way back." Jill decided that she liked the brown-eyed, fair-haired Jane.

They passed through the pony field, after climbing through the hedge. Jill tore her skirt, and said " bother ". Peter looked at Pat, and shrugged slightly.

" I say," said Jill, " what's the chestnut gelding called?"

" That's Sunny, my new pony," said Pat. " The brown gelding is Freddy, whom you can have to ride."

Jill looked at her and wondered if Pat thought Freddy was no good.

" Hm, thanks," said Jill. " He's got good hocks. I bet he can jump. But the bay's beautiful too." She looked, questioning, wondering about his name and who owned him.

" He's Bracken, my pony," said Peter, grinning at Jill's attempt to talk as if she understood.

" Is the brown mare yours, John?" she asked, turning to the sunburnt little boy.

" Oh yes." He turned away rudely.

" I ride Silver, the grey mare," said Jane, tucking her short hair behind her ears.

" She's quite young, isn't she?"

" Yes, only six," answered Jane.

" Do you want to look at her teeth?" asked John abruptly.

" No, thanks," replied Jill, " I can tell age before seven or after ten. The black marks are all that I know." She wanted to show that she knew something.

" Do you know those?" asked Pat, incredulous and scornful.

" Well, the groom told us once, at school. I've almost forgotten." Jill grinned bravely, but felt unhappy at Pat's contempt.

.   .   .   .

After tea Jill went round the house and gardens with Jane. They talked about school, and got on very well. Jill began to feel a little better.

Pat and Peter sat on the wall round the terrace, and watched Jill's progress round the garden.

" She's pretty awful," said Pat.

" We might be able to make something of her," Peter said, with his hands at the back of his neck.

" I doubt it," Pat retorted angrily.

" Well, she couldn't see Sandra properly." Peter liked Jill, rather, and wanted to give her a chance.

" *I* could. Of course, she's only just come, we'll have to give her a chance."

" She yelled at that nettle too. Still, we've got hardened to them."

" Hullo," said John, as he scrambled up beside them. " Isn't she weird?" His face beamed with energy.

" Pretty awful."

" I'd love to see her ride."

" Same here; let's go over and suggest it." Peter swung down and went over to Jill and Jane.

The girls heard his step, and turned to meet him.

Jill agreed to the ride at once, and dashed in to get her shorts on.

When she came down, the others were looking at a Horse Show schedule, and eagerly discussing it.

" Silver can't bend yet," Jane was saying. " She's much too wild. Do you like shows, Jill?"

" What, Horse Shows? I've never been in one." Jill looked at the schedule. " What's bending?"

" Don't you know that?" asked John. " Cantering in and out of a line of posts. You can try it on Freddy." He giggled, and the others smiled. Freddy was good at it, and very headstrong.

" What's pig-sticking, then?"

" One person drags a sack behind him at a gallop, and the first to stab it wins."

" But how——?"

Pat and John burst into laughter, and Peter, glaring at them, grabbed a bridle and swung out of the yard. He hated quarrels, and feared that one might start.

CHAPTER III

Accidents

" Come and have a ride," said Jane to Jill. They walked down to the fields, each swinging a bridle, and thinking her own thoughts.

" Here are the ponies," said Jane. " Can you catch Freddy while I get Silver?"

Jill approached Freddy, and murmured softly to him. The pony came up and nosed around for carrots. Jill slipped the reins round his neck and got the bit into his mouth. She buckled the throat-lash, and turned round to see that Jane was having trouble with Silver.

" I can't bridle her in the field," Jane said. " I shall have to lead her in." The two girls walked up to the stables again and saddled the ponies. Pat and John slid out as they came in, bridles in hand. They talked softly and intently all the way down to the field, concocting some plan.

Jill mounted Freddy and adjusted her stirrups. Jane soon followed her example, and they rode out side by side. Silver curvetted and chinked her double bit. Freddy wore a snaffle and moved quietly.

They trotted down the track which served as a drive, took the road until they came to the beginning of a track through the woods, and then cantered up this. Freddy hopped nimbly over small, fallen branches, and pulled for his bit.

" Freddy's rather fresh," said Jane. " He hasn't been ridden much."

" I think he's lovely," said Jill.

" Pat says she's tired of him."

They cantered on, holding the eager ponies in, until they came to a hidden fork in the path. There, suddenly and unexpectedly, Pat and John came up galloping, and brushed past Freddy, who was in the lead.

Silver backed away suddenly, as Freddy shied and kicked out. Jill, not expecting the sudden stop, flew over his head and landed on her side. Pat turned back at this, and spoke scornfully.

" I'm sorry. Freddy did behave unusually badly."

Jill smarted, both from her fall and the hint. Pat had emphasized " unusually ". Jane helped Jill on again, holding the excited Freddy.

" You should ride him more often," she said to Pat, rather coldly. Pat stared at her and flushed. Then she suggested that they should join forces. Jane agreed reluctantly.

Jill trotted after them, feeling depressed at the ructions she had caused between these friends.

The track eventually led out into the open, and climbed steeply in zigzags to the top of the ridge. They urged the panting ponies up to the top, and let them have a breather, tethered to a small shrub, with loosened girths.

Pat led the others to a vantage point, and they all gazed round at the fine view. The moors swelled away all around them, peaked and gigantic, though they were not quite so high to the north-west, an indication that the rocks were softer and not pure granite.

In the valley beneath them they could see the fields belonging to Pat's house, and the stream which ran through them.

" What's that house farther down the valley?" asked Jill.

"That's Appleby's place," said Pat. "He's the local farmer; not that we buy much from him, except pork and bacon."

They turned round and gazed into the next valley. It was wide, and not very deep. A ledge ran above it, about twenty feet from the top, from which the ground sloped gently down, but the descent from the top to this ledge was steep and precipitous. Broken rock and stones littered the slope, and only a few straggly clumps of heather covered its nakedness.

"I say, let's go down to that ledge," said John.

"Oh no," Jane started, "it's too——"

"I bet you daren't, Jill," Pat cut in, thinking she would be afraid.

"I jolly well will," said Jill hotly, and shaking off Jane's restraining hand, she plunged towards the ledge before anyone could stop her.

Jill started down the slope carefully, working in diagonals, and took advantage of the heather and the firmer rocks. She tore her hand on a jagged piece, however, as she stretched for another handhold. As she sucked the cut, her right foot began to slide, and when she grabbed for the nearest heather to steady herself, it gave way, and she slid towards the bottom without anything to catch hold of.

Jill tried to dig her heels in, to hold on to a plant or to a rock, but the rock gave way and scraped a groove down her leg. She did succeed in slowing down a little, which softened the landing at the bottom. The girl lay there for a moment, then got up and waved when those at the top yelled down to her. They couldn't see her for the dust she had raised. She examined her wounds, and wondered how to get up again.

She had a bad cut on her leg, and several on her arms,

besides many bruises, but nothing was actually broken or twisted.

As she looked round, wondering what to do, Peter rode up bareback on Bracken, having seen the descent from farther up the valley, where he had been riding by himself and trying to sort out his feelings. He rather liked Jill, and yet she appeared so silly and namby-pamby.

He put these thoughts aside now, as she was in difficulty, and dismounted to help her.

" What happened?" he asked.

" I tried to climb down, and slipped," Jill explained, catching her breath as she realized she was near tears.

" Well, you get up on Bracken, and I'll lead you round an easier way," he said kindly, smiling—" unless you've broken anything?"

" No, I don't think so," said Jill.

He gave her an easy leg-up, and led Bracken up the valley until they could get to the ridge again.

" You're jolly brave," he said. " That's a nasty cut."

" It doesn't hurt much," said Jill, sounding more cheerful than she felt.

When they got back to the others, they found Pat looking very white.

" I didn't really mean that ' dare '," she said. " You were awfully brave to attempt it."

Mrs. Hever was very shocked when they got home, and put Jill to bed immediately she had seen to the damage.

Jill did not mind so much; she had a nice time with the other four wandering round her, and playing Monopoly or card games. It was Pat who got the worst of it, for when she confessed that she had " dared " Jill to do it, her mother was very annoyed, and threatened to stop her riding, the one thing Pat loved. Pat felt resentful, and considered that Jill should have said something to ease the blame.

. . . .

The next morning Jill was very stiff, and Mrs. Hever decreed another day in bed.

Jill was rather sorry, but the others promised to see that one of them at least was up there the whole time, to keep her amused, which Jill thought very handsome, and said so.

" Oh, well," said Pat, " I don't mind at all, because Mum says I can't ride."

" Not because of last night?" asked Jill.

" Yes. Well, it was my fault, and I'm terribly sorry."

" Oh no, Pat. I shouldn't have done it. It was my own risk. After all, one needn't accept a ' dare '."

" But I know how you feel about it, Jill. I should hate to refuse one, as you would." Pat decided that she rather liked Jill, but still found her presence irritating.

When Mrs. Hever came up to see how Jill was, Jill tried to open up the subject of Pat's riding.

" It wasn't Pat's fault last night." She decided to get to the point quickly. " Pat was only joking."

" Don't take the blame for it, Jill. She shouldn't joke like that with a new guest."

" Yes, but I should hate to feel she couldn't ride because of me."

" Why, that's sweet of you, Jill! Well, I'll let her ride to-morrow, but she must have some punishment, so that she doesn't do it again."

Mrs. Hever smiled at Jill, thinking that a forgiving nature was a very pleasant virtue.

" Yes, I think you can get up to lunch, but you must stay in the house to-day, so that you don't gallop around and open up that leg again. It's healing nicely now."

Peter came in and asked how Jill felt. Mrs. Hever slipped
off to see about lunch. She had daily help in the house, but
she couldn't find anyone who wanted to live so far out, and
anyway, she preferred to cook herself, as she was a really
good hand at it.

Peter and Jill played German whist, until John and Jane
joined them. Jill won three games, and Peter four.

John suggested Monopoly, and so Peter went and fetched
it. Pat came up with him, and they all five played until Jane
ran out of money and had to mortgage all her property.
They all felt sick of it by then, and packed it up.

"Those games always last too long," said Peter. "I
know, let's make one of our own that's a bit quicker."

"Oo, yes," said John, "a racing one."

"On the flat," said Jill, getting excited. Peter went and
got some cardboard and pencils. Pat produced a pair of
strong scissors and a pair of compasses.

They had got the outline of the racecourse marked out,
a fairly regular oval, and were discussing the rules and
method of the game.

"Let's have six horses each, and a certain sum of money,"
said Peter, "and then have six different length races in one
game. One of them could be a selling-plate, you know,
where the winner is put to auction afterwards."

"And each horse is worth a certain amount to start with
and is worth more each time it gets placed." Pat's brain
took hold of the idea.

"The person with the most money or value of money at
the end wins," finished John. They all grinned, and Mrs.
Hever called that it was nearly lunch-time.

.   .   .   .

The next day Jill felt very well, and was champing to

get about again, so Mrs. Hever said that she could go out, as long as she didn't ride Freddy, or run too fast.

"I'm going to give Prince a bit more training this morning," Mrs. Hever said at breakfast, "so you can all come and watch him, if you like."

"Oh, how super!" said Peter. "I want to learn how to train them when they're more difficult, so that I can be a trainer at Newmarket."

"Do you really want to, Peter?" asked Jill. "I bet it's hard work."

"Yes, but it's worth it," said Peter, with vigour.

The children sat on the fence of the field where the jumps and bending-posts were, and Mr. Hever mounted Nagina, Prince's mother, in case Mrs. Hever wanted any help, for she had never yet been able to mount Prince.

"Oh, isn't he perfectly lovely!" said Jill, as the three-year-old colt was led into the field, with arched neck, and limbs moving in regular cadency, his tail held high and sweeping. He was a rich, deep black, with blue lights in his shining coat.

"Yes," said Peter, "he's pedigree Arab."

Mrs. Hever led Prince round the track which had been worn in the grass during his training. He set his feet down lightly and carefully, holding himself proudly, with dignity. Jill followed him with her eyes, feeling his every movement, caught by the poetry of his perfect action. The young animal trotted and cantered at Mrs. Hever's command, while she stood in the centre of his circle.

She backed him, still with the lungeing reins, and made him passage. She then made the colt circle again.

"Okay, Bill," she said, and her husband brought up two jumps, which he placed on the track, on opposite sides of the circle. They were plain, two-foot bars.

PRINCE IS BEING EDUCATED

"He jumps naturally," said Mrs. Hever as she turned Prince loose, and sat on the fence beside the children.

Mr. Hever cantered past the grazing pony, who followed his mother, and when Nagina was put over a high brush jump, about three feet high, Prince followed.

"I've often seen him gallop over a jump by himself," said Mrs. Hever, "only he never tackles a white jump. He prefers natural obstacles, like the brush or a plain bar, unwhitewashed."

Prince galloped up to them, and they gave him sugar or carrots or apples. He was friendly with Jill, and pressed his nose into her knee, nearly knocking her off the fence.

"He likes you," Mrs. Hever informed Jill.

"I like him too," Jill replied.

"I say," said Jane, "let's hold a Horse Show for Jill to watch."

"That's a good idea, Jane." Mrs. Hever jumped off the fence. "Jill can learn best by example."

Mrs. Hever agreed to judge them, and wrote down the schedule. Jill sat on the fence, and petted Prince while they contested for Best Rider, Jumping, Bending and Obstacle Race and Potato Race.

"Taking age into consideration, I think John is the best," said Mrs. Hever. "We won't find second and third."

Peter won the Jumping easily on Bracken, and the Bending, but the pony played up in the other classes, and Pat won the Potato Race, while Jane's Silver galloped to the front in the Obstacle Race.

Jill watched with great interest, her arm round the quiet Prince's neck.

CHAPTER IV

Conquests

Jill opened her eyes and blinked sleepily around her, then turned over and dozed again. After a while, the soft, insistent sound which had woken her before, penetrated the thick walls of sleep, and she rolled on to her back, and lay there, gazing at the ceiling.

It suddenly occurred to her that it was rather dark. She glanced at the clock by her bed. Seven o'clock already, so she jumped out of bed and went to the window. Before she was half-way there, she realized that it was raining.

"Oh!" she said, and stared in horror at the scene, so vastly changed from its former smiling warmth.

The moors rolled away bleakly, lost in mist, and the rain drove from the west in raw gusts. Jill shivered and returned to the protection of her warm bed. Even there she could see the heavy, colourless sky hanging grimly, low on the tors, and drifting into the valleys.

Pat and Jane came in, knocking, but not waiting for Jill's reply.

"How beastly!" said Pat. "We shall have to stay indoors."

"The poor ponies!" sighed Jane.

"Oh, they have to get used to it," said Pat. "Even the hunters are out now, as it's summer."

Jill felt warmed by the company of her own kind, and

was confident enough to laugh at her previous fear of the elements.

The three girls dressed, and hammered on the boys' door to get them up. As it was still early, they decided to go down and see their ponies, to cheer up the wet animals. Peter had brought his mac with him, so he raided the larder for sugar while the others got their macs. They all wore gym shoes, with no socks.

The high grass between the fields brushed against their legs and threw cold drops into their faces as they ran to warm their numbed feet, slipping about considerably. The ponies were bunched under the trees, backs to the wind, and rolling their jaws patiently. Without the protection of the high hedges each side of the lane, the children's macs flapped disconsolately in the wind, and soon became wet inside, as well as out.

When Jill had petted Freddy, and given him his sugar-lumps, she turned to see that Prince had come up silently, and was waiting behind her. She fondled him, rubbed the rain off his shoulder, and pulled his ears gently until they were warm. Prince submitted to this, and nickered as Jill spoke to him.

" Gosh," said John, " I'm freezing! Let's go back." They said a fond farewell to their ponies, Jill to Freddy *and* Prince, and raced up to the house, where they dried out as quickly as possible before Mrs. Hever saw them. At breakfast, they appeared as usual, as if they had not been outside.

.   .   .   .

" Well, you can play ball-games in the barn. Daddy has put the ping-pong table in the one opposite the garage one. Oh, well, you know what I mean." Mrs. Hever ended with the table in laughter at her redundancy.

The children raced over to the barn, and played a tournament, as there was an odd number of players for table-tennis. First of all, Jill played Jane, the winner played John, and that winner played the winner of the game between Peter and Pat.

Jill played carefully with Jane, and kept an early lead of three points to win. Next Pat played Peter, and they were almost level up to ten-all, but then Peter got a lead of three, making the score 14–11, to Peter. Pat played with more care, and the score crept to 15–14, still to Peter. Peter then began to lash out, and lost two points quickly. Pat began to place the balls dangerously near the edge, and did not gain more than she lost that way. The score was then 17–18, Peter's service, and they both played slowly and stolidly, prolonging the suspense of the spectators. In the end, Pat won by one point. Jill managed to return John's very erratic serves, and gave him some tricky ones, to win easily by five points.

Then it was Jill and Pat to play in the finals. They faced each other coolly as Peter tossed for service. Jill won the toss. They both played with reserve up to half-way, when Pat led by one point, but then Jill began to demonstrate her brilliant, original style, which her father had noticed and encouraged. The score shot up to 17–12, Jill's service, and Pat began to feel very frustrated and jealous. Jill noticed that her opponent looked rather piqued, and decided to let her win, for the sake of some peace.

The others, watching, could see that Jill had complete control of the game and that she lost on purpose, and clapped very loud. Pat looked pleased and suggested playing pig in the middle, with three pigs.

" If you'd like to," she said to Jill. " *You* are the guest."

" Oh yes, let's," said Jill eagerly.

They pushed the table to one side and cast lots.

" Peter and I are outside," said Jane, after examining the bits of paper.

" I'm middle pig," said Jill.

" That's most difficult," said Peter. " You'll have to jump up."

Peter and Jane threw the ball to each other, but none of the pigs could get near it. Jane, laughing at their antics, suddenly threw the ball almost into Pat's hands by mistake. A few minutes later, Pat threw a fast-dropping one, which John managed to catch.

A few minutes later, Peter threw a high one, which Jane couldn't quite reach, but Jill jumped, and just got it. Most of the throws were practically on the roof.

" At last," said Pat as Jill took Peter's place. Jill stuck out her tongue in answer.

After a little more of that, they all felt fed up with it, and sat on the table, swinging their legs.

" I know," said Jane suddenly, " let's do some jumping."

" Gosh, yes!" said Peter. He found some nails in a tin can, and they banged a few at regular intervals into a jutting beam at one side of the barn.

" What else can we use?" asked Jill, looking round.

Peter tied two sticks together in a cross, and leant another up against them. It stood quite firm, and so he took it down and banged similar nails into the upright stick.

They balanced a round, thin pole on two nails, and jumped it in turn. Peter put down their names in his note-book, and left a space to write the highest jump they cleared. Pat and the three from India always preferred to jump from the front, as they said it put them off riding over jumps straight, if they didn't, but Jill's father had taught her to jump in the more professional way, as he had been a great athlete himself. She therefore preferred to jump from the side, and always did so at school, but here there was no room, so she had to jump straight.

John's limit was 2 ft. 8 in., and as they were pretty hot by then, they took off their sandals to cool their feet. Peter decided to jump barefoot, and the girls followed his example.

Jill was out at 3 ft. 3 in., and Pat was scornful.

" You're not much of a jumper," she said aggressively.

" No," Jill agreed pleasantly, " I prefer to jump sideways."

" Oh, la-di-da!" Pat picked up Jill's sandal and twiddled it round her finger. Jill leapt on her, but Pat rushed for the door, and as Jill emerged into the rain, Pat hurled the shoe on to the roof of the barn-garage.

" You rotter!" said Jill, glaring.

" Go and fetch it, then," said Pat, grinning, and darting out of reach.

Jill ran to the rain butt, and leapt on to its rim, where she balanced. The roof of the bike- and tool-shed was within reach, so she grabbed at the edge, and swung her knee on to it. She slowly wriggled on and stood up. The roof of the barn was only about five feet away, but being thatched, the edge where it jutted was almost unsupported, and not safe. Jill located her sandal, which had lodged a few feet up the thatching, and decided that she must jump for it. Peter, seeing her intentions, yelled to her.

" Don't be such an ass!" he screeched. " It isn't safe." She waved her hand to them and leapt. She landed on hands and knees, and sprawled. Her hand closed over the sandal as the thatch began to disintegrate, and she soon landed on the ground amid a shower of dust and wet straw. Luckily the barn was quite low, and Jill was not hurt. She scrambled up at once and showed the sandal to Pat, who sneered.

JILL TAKES A DARE

When Mrs. Hever found out, she was very cross. She asked why Jill had gone up there, and Jill quickly said that it was her own idea. Peter was told that he should have stopped Jill, and that they must help to mend the roof. Pat stayed silent, which shocked the other four, but they said nothing.

·   ·   ·   ·   ·   ·   ·   ·   ·

A few days later, at breakfast, Mr. Hever looked up from his paper, and cleared his throat.

" I was over at Martins' yesterday," he said, " and they say you can use their swimming-pool while they're away."

" Oh, good!" said Pat. " I say, Peter, it would be fun. The Martins are friends of ours, and only live about five miles away."

" You can take a picnic this afternoon," said Mrs. Hever, " but you mustn't mess their pool up with sticks or paper-bags, remember. And I shouldn't lie about in wet suits unless the sun's pretty hot, or you'll be in bed with colds to-morrow."

The children promised to be good, and after lunch they mounted their ponies and trotted off down the road, knap-sacks bumping on their backs. After what seemed like miles of road, they turned off over the moor, and cut across to a valley where a large house stood, with a swimming-pool near by.

Five minutes later they were all jumping in, and de-lighting in the feeling of the cool, soft water after their hot ride. The ponies they had turned into a handy paddock, where they could see them. Peter did two lengths on his back, and then tried to swim under water, while the others watched; Jane and Jill practised different strokes and chatted about the ponies. Pat and John had a splashing match, and then conferred together softly.

Suddenly Jill felt her legs being pulled from under her, and struggled. She came up gasping, and swam as fast as she could towards Pat, who was splashing with huge sweeps of her arm, and incidentally, with fair accuracy. Jane followed her more slowly, sending sprays of the water over John, who was behind them.

A huge battle of water-splashing started, and Peter

climbed to the top-board, so that he could watch better. He wanted to join in, but didn't know which side to take.

Jill concentrated on reaching Pat and ducking her, but the flying water was confusing, and she kept losing sight of her enemy in the excitement and muddle. Once or twice Pat felt a hand on her shoulder, and when Jill, in desperation, trying underwater tactics, nearly got a grip on Pat's ankle, the latter deemed it time to beat a hasty retreat, and she and John raced to the side.

Jane swam up to the deep end, and Jill followed. They floated there, looking up at Peter on the diving-board.

"Look out!" said the sunburned boy, getting up. "I'm going to dive!" Jane and Jill moved nearer the side and Peter did a really graceful swallow-dive, with a clean entry. When he came up, he swam over to them and also floated, though jerkily.

"Can you dive?" he suddenly asked Jill.

"Well, yes, off the edge," she replied, "but not as well as you can."

"Have a go off the edge, then," Jane suggested.

Jill climbed out, panting as she wriggled over the stone edge. She stood up and prepared to dive, ignoring Pat and John, who stood laughing near by. Jill felt very angry with them, but kept it to herself.

As she dived, however, John sprang forward and pulled her leg sideways, so that she landed on her back. The water stung, and she went under with the shock of it.

"Ya!" said Pat as Jill came up, "you can't even dive off the edge!"

Jill's temper boiled, and she felt like drowning Pat. Instead, she swam up to the diving-board, and climbed to the top. She looked at the water, and climbed down to the middle board. John shrieked and uttered scalding remarks.

Jill leapt off without a word, and hit the water with a resounding smack. When she came up, Peter yelled:

" Race you to the other end !"

They both shot off, doing a racy crawl, but Jill's was more efficiently used, and Peter couldn't help rolling a little, so he lost.

" I say, you've some spunk, and you *can* swim well," he said, panting and shaking the water out of his ears and eyes.

" So can you, except that you roll too much in the crawl. I can't dive at all."

" Well, let's teach each other, then." Peter grinned, and Jill agreed to the idea. They spent the rest of the afternoon chatting together as they practised the crawl and dives.

.   .   .   .

Jill and Peter were leaning over the fence, watching Prince eat some hay they had brought him.

" He's lovely," said Peter. " I wish I could ride him, but even Mrs. Hever can't get on him. He's too proud."

" What a shame !" said Jill. " What's the matter, then, Prince," she called out to the pony; " don't you want to go out for rides, and win prizes at shows, then?" Prince looked up and whinnied to her, then fed again.

" I say, he spoke to you," Peter said, amazed.

" Yes, he always answers me."

Jill climbed over the fence and went to pet Prince. He nuzzled her pocket for sugar, and rubbed his head on her arm.

" I see him twice a day." Jill turned and smiled at Peter. " I can lift his hooves now."

" He likes you more than anybody," said Peter, surprised and admiring her skill.

CHAPTER V

Arabs

Jill picked up a pile of seven plates, and carried them into the dining-room.

"Now," she thought—"Corn Flakes, plates, milk—oh, blow! The sugar!" She dashed into the kitchen, nearly knocking Pat over as she came in bearing butter and marmalade.

"Jill!" Peter came into the kitchen suddenly, his hair untidy, with no shoes on, but with a weighty parcel in one hand and some letters in the other.

"A parcel for you, Jill," he said. "Do see what's inside it!"

Jill leapt on it and began to untie the knots.

"Oh, cut it!" said Pat impatiently. "We do want to see it."

"Never cut string," explained Jill as she pulled at the tight knots. "It's a book," she said, with her parcel open at last.

"Gosh, what a whopper!" Peter gasped as a dictionary-sized volume appeared, with a blue cover, and some mystic signs on the front.

"Doesn't it look dry?" said Jill as she flicked through the pages. "*Seven Pillars of Wisdom*. That's a queer name. It sounds as though it's a good educational book."

They all laughed, and Mrs. Hever came in.

"Did I hear you say *Seven Pillars of Wisdom*?" she

asked. " That's a very interesting book, about the Arabs in the 1914 war."

" Arabs! Is it about their horses much?" Peter was interested.

" No, they rode camels mostly," Mrs. Hever replied.

" Here's the letter with it," said Jill. " I'll read it. ' Dear Jill, I hope you are well and enjoying yourself. Your mother and I are having a very good time. I saw this book the other day, and I thought you might be interested in it. Of course, some of it is very boring, but the parts about the Arab tribes and characters are fun, and the adventures that Lawrence gets up to are most original. You're probably much too busy riding and picnicking, from the sound of your letters, to bother with the book, but it might be useful on a wet day. Don't knock it about too much, as we want to read it when we get back.' That's about all," Jill finished.

" Is it fighting and charging?" John asked.

" It sounds like it," said Jill. " Here's a map. Jeddah. That's a town. Lawrence's journeys? Oh, I see."

They all crowded round. Surprisingly enough, they seemed to be quite enthusiastic about it. They peered at the pictures, laughed at the author's replies to editor's notes at the beginning, and wondered what happened in the book.

Mr. Hever came in then, so they had breakfast. After that, Peter went to the door and inspected the weather.

" I'm afraid it's going to rain," he said. " The sky's black as anything."

Everyone went to the door then, and they agreed with him.

" You'd better go to your barn, then, but no roof-climbing," warned Mrs. Hever.

The children went into the barn, Jill with the book under her arm.

" I say," said Jane——

" I know what you're going to say," said Peter.

" Let's be Arabs!" Jane continued triumphantly. They all nodded their heads and grinned.

" What tribe shall we be?" asked Pat, twirling round on one foot. She felt exhilarated and Eastern.

" I think we could keep our horses in here," said Peter, " so I think we'd better get them before it starts to rain."

" But how can we?" asked John.

" Well, there's room, and they could stay here in the day, anyway."

They ran down the well-worn path, and haltered their ponies. Jill spoke to Prince, and gave him his accustomed carrot. She thought him the most lovely thing she had ever seen, but she kept her love to herself.

In the barn, they roped off five squares, and tied their ponies to the rope farthest from the wall. The animals were about six feet from each other, which seemed a safe distance. Then Peter produced paper and a pencil, and they looked through the book for a tribal name.

" This sounds nice," said Jane. " How about the Juheina?"

" How's it spelt? Oh, I see."

" Yes, that's jolly good," said Pat.

They stopped talking and read a couple of chapters, craning round each other's heads.

" Bags being Feisal," said Peter, looking up.

" I want to be Abd el Kerim, then," said Jane, standing up and jigging on one foot.

" Oh! Oh, well, I bags be Abdulla el Deleimi." John quickly saw another name, and gave up all idea of Jane's choice.

" I don't know what to be," said Jill.

"Neither do I—Oh, this one's good—I'll be Auda Abu Tay." Pat saw a description of this war-like chief, and decided quickly.

"You can make one up out of two others, Jill," said Peter.

"Oh yes. Well, I think Rasim, and—I know! Rasim ibn Rualla!"

Peter rapidly scribbled their names on a sheet of paper he had with him, and wrote the names of their horses next to them.

"We ought to have pedigrees for them, O Feisal," said Jill in a queer nasal voice.

"They don't talk like that," said Pat.

"All right! Anyway, I bags being a racehorse breeder, and then all our horses are from my stud-farm." Jill was intensely interested in racing, and would have liked to be able to breed her own horses and to race them.

John at once spoke up.

"I'll ride them," he said. It was his one ambition, to be a jockey. He certainly had the talent.

"I'm going to train them, then," said Peter, who, being too heavy to be a jockey, had resigned himself to the lesser ambition of becoming a trainer.

"I want to just hack them about," said Jane, "but I could do portraits of them." The thing that Jane loved about horses was their beauty and their friendliness, the way they pushed their noses into her arm, and the wonderful co-ordination of their movements. As she had some skill at drawing and painting, it was her ambition to become a famous animal portrait-painter, like George Stubbs.

Pat, having been taught from an early age the care of a horse, felt that she would like to be a veterinary surgeon, and to relieve animals' suffering.

" I'll vet. them," she said, " and see that they're fit for morning exercise."

" I never thought you were interested in racing or anything, Rasim," said John, wonder in his voice.

" Oh, golly, yes!" Jill exclaimed. " I love racehorses."

Peter said that the barn must be the Arab camp, and therefore richly decorated, so they hunted for old rugs, to hang up as tapestry.

That afternoon, when they had ransacked the attics for some furniture to put in their camp, they sat back and surveyed their work. They had found two good orange boxes, one sagging one, two three-legged chairs, about two-thirds of a stool, and an old moth-eaten pouffe. These they grouped at the far end of the barn, so that the horses had room to be led into the stalls.

" We shall have to be trained as Arabs first," Peter maintained, " and then we can go out and fight the cowardly old Turks."

" Rah !" screamed the others.

" How are we to be trained," asked Pat, " and who is going to train us?"

" I am," said Peter firmly, " and we'll have to learn to vault on and off, fight on horseback, and tent-peg."

" What's tent-pegging?"

" You gallop along, and try to stab a handkerchief, or something, with a javelin," John informed the seeker.

" It does sound fun," said Jill.

" Yes, but rather difficult," added Jane.

" Oh no, not really," said Pat, feeling jealous of Jill's new popularity, but not knowing what to do about it.

　　　·　　·　　·　　·　　·　　·　　·　　·　　·

After tea Mrs. Hever decided that the weather had

cleared up enough to begin Prince's training of carrying a rider.

" Can I try him, Mum?" asked Pat, very excited.

" Oh, I don't think so, Pat. Not yet. He's very sensitive, and knows me better than you. Besides, unless you do a bit more towards looking after him, you'll never be able to do anything with him."   Mrs. Hever had said that Pat could have Prince for her own, if she did all the grooming and feeding, but Pat had not kept it up, and the horse did not trust her very well.

Peter carried the bridle and saddle down to Prince's field, and sat on the gate with the others while Mrs. Hever saddled the colt.

" I'll mount him here," she called to them; " come and give me a hand, Peter."

Peter went and held the animal's head while Mrs. Hever pulled up the girths, which made Prince wince a little. Then she put her foot into the stirrup, and swung lightly into the saddle.

For a moment Prince stood still, then he realized the weight on his back, and down went his head and up went his heels.   Mrs. Hever gripped hard and hung on to his mane.   He reared suddenly, and still the fine horsewoman kept on, seeking to contact his mouth and to make him obedient.   Then, however, he bucked.   He went through a whole series of twisting, shivering shocks.

Mrs. Hever flew in a graceful circle after the third buck, and landed on her side.

" Don't touch him yet," she called to the children, looking on rather horrified at these proceedings.

" Are you all right?" asked Pat, coming forward anxiously.   Prince stopped bucking, looked at Mrs. Hever in surprise, and came over to sniff at her.

PRINCE SHOWS HE CAN BUCK

"Yes, I'm all right, dear," she said, patting Prince's neck and scrambling to her feet. "Come on, Peter, we'll try again."

She led the colt round until he had cooled off, and then

mounted in the same way as before. As soon as Peter let go of the bridle at a nod from Mrs. Hever, Prince again bucked violently, and again succeeded in dislodging his rider, who landed rather harder. Prince galloped to the far end of the field, and there tried to shake off his saddle. Mrs. Hever staggered to her feet this time, and compressed her lips tightly.

" I think I've broken my arm," she said, and not feeling able to say any more, went on up to the house with Jane and Pat. Jill and Peter wanted to go with them, but Mrs. Hever managed to say, " Don't forget Prince," and so they stayed to see if they could get the saddle off him. John still sat on the fence, very shocked, and not quite taking in what was happening.

After some time Jill managed to calm Prince enough to take off his tack, and the two friends left him quiet and happy again, quite unaware of the damage and confusion he had caused.

Mrs. Hever was put to bed with her arm in plaster, after the doctor had come and declared it to be a clean break, which would soon mend.

CHAPTER VI

A Daring Plan

During the next few days, the children stayed in or about the house, in case they should be needed. Mrs. Hever did not feel well enough to cook or move about much, so the girls cooked the meals and gave her breakfast in bed. Later she would get up at her leisure and sit in the garden reading.

Mr. Hever was very busy at this time of year, and had little time to look after his horses. Peter offered to see that they were fed and groomed and exercised, and every one of the children had some job in the stable. Peter and Pat had to ride two of the hunters round the fields for an hour, and also lead one of the Arabs each at the same time.

John and Jane rode Doricles and Firefly, as these animals were a little smaller than Ben and Sandra, but Jill had nothing to ride but the ponies, and so she rode Freddy round the fields with the others, and thus learnt a lot about horses, riding, and particularly about Freddy. She began to get really good at handling him, and could understand his whims better than the others.

In the afternoon Mrs. Hever came down to the practice field once or twice, and gave them hints on their riding. There was to be a Horse Show at the end of August, and the children were practising hard for it. Jill learnt to jump show jumps, finding in Freddy an excellent mount for a nervous, imperfect rider.

By the end of a week Jill could jump as high as the others,

and had gained much respect from them, for her promising ability.

. . . .

"Children," said Mrs. Hever one morning at breakfast, "there's a race meeting at Princetown next week. Would you like to go?" She was feeling quite herself again now, but of course her arm was in plaster still, and she was under strict orders not to ride yet.

"Ooh! yes, please!" Pat was excited, and John simply shrieked with delight. After they had cleared up breakfast, Jill and Peter decided that it was going to be a hot day, and the other three readily agreed to the idea of a bathe in the river which lay at the bottom of their field.

It was quite high, as it had been such a wet summer, and it also had several fine, deep pools which were big enough for quite a good swim. Of course, one had to go round and round in a circle, but still, it was water, and above all, cool and wet.

They ran down in their bathing costumes, promising to be back by 11.30, so that they could get dry, and then have lunch ready by one o'clock. John was the first in, closely followed by the other four. For a little while they splashed round, bemoaning the fact that their friends of the bathing pool had returned, and were therefore using the said pool themselves.

"Oh, well," said Jill, "it's a long way to go anyhow."

"Yes, by the time you get back you're as hot as you were before," added Jane. They floated in silence for a while, content with their thoughts, and with the cool water on their hot limbs.

"I say," said Peter, suddenly standing up, "what's the time?" He looked at the watch on his wrist.

"Oh, you ass!" said Jane in agonized tones. "That's

the third time you've ruined a watch by forgetting to take it off when you swim."

"Oh, hang!" said Peter. "Well, I'm not going to just give it up this time. I bet it won't hurt it; I'll take it to bits this afternoon and dry it before it begins to rust." He took it off, shook it, and laid it on the bank.

"You know what happened the last time you tried to take it to bits," warned Jane.

"Well, why shouldn't he?" asked John. "It's better than——"

"Oh, stop squabbling!" said Pat, flicking water at John. That started a water-fight, which lasted for many fierce minutes, until a figure appeared in the distance, approaching rapidly and roaring with rage.

"Look out, here's Appleby, the farmer next door to us. He hates children." Pat leapt out of the water as she spoke, and began to gather up towels. Then the five sprinted towards the house, hoping that Appleby would not pursue them.

"Ye young brats!" he shouted, panting, his normally rosy countenance flushed with rage and excitement. "You may own that bit of the river, but my farm's downstream from yours, and if you stir up the water, it's all muddy for my cows to drink. Don't let me catch ye at these games again!" He was a Scotsman, and had red hair and the usual temper which accompanies it, not at all sweetened by thirty years of hard work, battling against nature and the weather to keep his farm going.

The children reached the house in safety, having left Appleby behind at the top of the first field. They got dried quickly, and then all took part in the complicated business of " getting lunch ".

That afternoon, while Jane and John helped Pat to

"YE YOUNG BRATS!"

61

exercise the horses, as Peter had excused himself from the work to mend his watch, he and Jill went to their camp, and started to dismember the unfortunate instrument.

" I say, is *that* what happens inside?" asked Jill in amazement, as Peter prized off the back and showed her the mechanism, which no one really understands except watchmakers, and young men trying to show off to young women, of course! At least, they always say they understand——

" You see, this wheel fits into that one, and turns it round, and then that makes this little lever twiddle over there, which turns that wheel this way, and so turns this wheel here." Peter sounded very confident, and Jill nodded her head intelligently.

Peter probed about amongst the wheels, and managed to detach two of them.

" It's going to be jolly good at the races," said Jill. " I've never seen any before."

" I have, in India," said Peter. " It's awfully good; you get lots of little ponies, terribly shaggy and stocky, which kick like anything. They start them more or less together, and gosh, do they go like the wind!"

" When did you leave India?" asked Jill, envious of the strange and wonderful memories these children had of foreign lands and people. She longed to travel, and her one definite ambition was to sail round the world.

" Oh, two years ago," said Peter. " It was when Jane caught typhoid. Our parents decided that the climate was too much for us, and we were all sent back to our aunt in Scotland. It was awful then, when Jane was so ill, and we couldn't see anyone for fear they caught the infection from us."

" Oh, how awful! Yes, it must have been boring and strange, too, in a new country," Jill said, realizing how lucky she was to have parents in England and a home with them.

"That's why Jane isn't much good at anything, because she hasn't been allowed to play games until this spring," Peter stuck up for his sister.

"Well, she rides very well if she's only just started. I've been riding for a year now."

"Is that all? You can manage the ponies jolly well. You've really got a way with Prince. I bet you could train him easily."

"Do you really think so?"

"Yes, why——"

"Yes! That's an idea." They stared at each other, a sudden inspiration in their eyes, a vision in their minds, making a bond of thought between them.

"We ought to train him between us, in secret." Jill's eyes glowed as she spoke.

"Where shall we train him? We ought to start now." Peter's mind worked quickly and foresaw the difficulties which lay before them.

"What time in the day can we do it?"

They were both silent for some minutes, but could find no solution to the problem.

"Early in the morning, I suppose, and any time the others are out of the way."

"Yes, that'll be best, then we can use the training field. We'll have to be jolly careful, though."

"Well, let's start now. We can go and halter him, and see how he responds to your leading." Peter got up as he spoke, heartlessly abandoning the ghastly remains of his watch, which he pushed into a pile and left on the box.

Jill ran into the harness-room and grabbed a halter. Then she hurried after Peter, who was already some way down the path.

When they got to Prince's field, they saw him standing under a tree, lazily swishing his tail at the flies, and not bothering to graze. He looked up as Jill approached, and prepared to gallop away.

" It's all right, Prince," she said, " don't be frightened."

And the horse allowed her to slip the halter over his ears. Once she had him thus secured, she gave him his usual apple. Peter came up and patted the fine black coat and talked soothingly. Then Jill led him round in a small circle.

" He leads okay, anyhow," she said. " He hardly notices the halter."

" No, he's already halter-broken. He doesn't like his back being touched, though."

Jill and Peter then stood on either side of the colt, and tried to rub his back firmly from withers to loins, but Prince backed away and nipped at them.

" That's no good," said Peter. " We'd better lead him a bit more."

So, for the next quarter of an hour, Jill led Prince round in circles, figures of eight, and squares, while Peter told her what to do. The colt obeyed her well, and rubbed his head against her arm now and again.

" We could train him any time in the day if it wasn't for the others," said Jill. " Shall we tell them?"

" Oh no. We mustn't tell anyone. The more people who know, the more dangerous it is."

" Dangerous?"

" Yes, of course, we shouldn't really play about with someone else's horse. I think we can do some good with him, though, that's why I'm doing it now."

" Gosh, I never thought."

" Well, I don't think we'll hurt him. We'll just have to train him when the others aren't around."

Jill felt worried about Peter's remark, but said nothing more, and gave her mind to leading the young Arab.

" Now back him," cried Peter, some twenty yards away. Jill pulled on the halter, and pressed his shoulder with her hand. The colt responded and leant back on his hocks, pulling his forefeet under him slowly and regularly.

" That's right! He does it jolly well," called Peter. " Now make him trot back here." The colt stepped out boldly, with his shoulders rippling as he thrust his forelegs before him. Jill ran by his side, the halter rope slack in her hand.

The two children stopped the training then, and stood admiring the animal's points, while he in turn watched their faces and wondered what they would do next.

" He's beautifully made, isn't he?" said Jill. " You wait until he goes in for shows—he'll win all the prizes."

She rapturously patted Prince's firmly curved neck, and pressed her face into his tumbled mane.

" I say, he does let you handle him a lot," said Peter. " At that rate it won't be long before you can mount him."

Jill slipped the halter off the Arab's head, and she and Peter walked up towards the house.

" What shall we do with him next?" asked Jill, turning to look at Peter as he came up the hill two paces behind her.

" Well, we'd better try to stroke his back until he's less tender. Then we can get him used to a saddle by slow degrees."

" Oh, I hope it doesn't take too long!" Jill was impatient for the day when she would feel the slim black withers between her knees, and the silky mouth at the end of her reins.

" It's no good hurrying, you know," said Peter. " He won't take long, though."

They walked silently, thinking of the beautiful grace of Prince, controlled and suppressed until he moved springily and with the minimum of effort. Peter wished that he should be the first to ride Prince, but could see that Jill had a great bond of sympathy with the colt.

" The races are on Wednesday, aren't they?" asked Jill suddenly.

" Yes, four more days yet. It's like waiting for Christmas. I bet it'll be super. I love racehorses." Peter thrilled in the expectation of joys to come.

" I wish we could race Prince," sighed Jill, " but that's impossible."

" There ought to be races for Arabs," said Peter thoughtfully. They went in to tea.

CHAPTER VII

The Army at Work

Jill woke suddenly, the next morning, before it was quite light.

"I wonder what woke me," she thought. "It's still quite early."

She got up and went to the window. She could see some ponies in the practice-field, dark shadows under the grey form of an oak. Behind them the ground sloped down to the hedge, and that hedge was so thick and high that the other fields were invisible. Farther away, the moors swept up and towered in irregular folds, crowned with sharp crags of bare granite. The lower slopes of the tors were drowned in a moving mist, which washed silently at the grey-green sides without making any impression. The birds were still asleep, and everything looked colourless and ghostly.

Jill shivered and got back into bed. Suddenly she felt miserable and homesick. This wild Dartmoor was so ugly and forbidding at times! The usually cheerful girl fell asleep again, crying softly to herself.

At seven o'clock, Jane knocked at Jill's door and burst in.

"I say," she said, sitting on the foot of the bed, "Peter says we're going to have an inspection of forces after breakfast, and that we'd better get the horses and tack cleaned up now. I'll go and get dressed, and meet you in five minutes." Jill blinked and nodded, and Jane dashed out again.

Jill turned over on to her back and stretched. She felt warm and happy, having completely forgotten how she had woken up earlier in the morning.

She sat up and swung her legs from under the blankets. The floor was damp with the mist that was floating in at the window, and Jill shivered, but quite cheerfully. She put on a warm jersey with her jodhpurs, and dashed along to the bathroom, where she splashed herself vaguely with water, and scratched inefficiently at her teeth, which ablutions were meant to represent her toilet. Then she swung out of the door, and bumped into Pat.

" Come on," said the latter; " Jane's ready, and Peter's down there already."

The two girls raced down the stairs, and stopped suddenly at the bottom when Jane, who was waiting there, motioned them to be quieter.

" Oh, gosh, of course! Mum's still asleep!" Pat glanced up the stairs.

" I say, wait for me!" John came out of his bedroom and slammed the door.

" Sh! John," said Jane. " Hurry up, but be quiet."

John walked downstairs quietly, but could not resist jumping the last four stairs, and slipped on a rug as he landed, almost knocking over a table which stood near.

" Oh, John, really!" said Jane, and then smiled. They straightened the rug and table, and tiptoed out of the back door, which made less noise when opened than the front door.

Once outside, they burst into a gallop, and raced each other down to the stables. Peter heard their feet on the stone yard and poked his head round the stable door.

" Hullo!" he said. " You down at last? Hurry up, I've almost finished Bracken."

All five spent the next half-hour grooming the ponies, cleaning out the stables, and polishing their saddles and bridles. As she was rubbing up Silver's bit, Jane suddenly said:

" Gosh, is it time for breakfast yet? It must be pretty late."

" Yes, it is, because I feel jolly hungry," said John.

The stable clock stood at twenty to four—and stayed there. It had stopped, in protest at Peter's efforts to wind it, the day before.

" It must be time to go up, anyway. You know how long it takes to get breakfast." Pat had had an unfortunate encounter with a scrambled egg the day before, when she had left it too long in the saucepan, and it had refused to come out. Breakfast had been an hour late!

" Why don't you help us with breakfast, Peter?" asked Jill. " Perhaps you won't grumble about a little bit of burn then."

" Ooh, yes! Can we help, Pat?" John bounced. " Can I fry the eggs?"

" Heaven preserve us!" ejaculated Peter, laughing, and they all trotted up to the house, for it had started to drizzle.

.   .   .   .

After breakfast that morning, Jill and Jane washed up, while Pat made the beds. Mrs. Hever came in as they were finishing the drying.

" Oh, there you are," she said. " I think we'd better have meat pudding for lunch, and fruit and custard. Now, that's quite easy. I've written the instructions on this bit of paper. By the way, you'll be glad to hear that I'm getting a cook. It isn't really fair on you to have to waste your holidays cooking."

" Oh, we don't mind," said Jill, " it's fun."

"Good! But still, when we get better weather, you'll want to go out more. The cook can finish off what house-work the woman doesn't do, too. Also, she'll be company for me at times, if I can manage to get the sort I want."

"Gosh, it's a good idea," said Jane, and Mrs. Hever withdrew, smiling.

"Hurry up, you girls!" yelled Peter from the hall. "It's time for inspection."

Pat ran downstairs and joined Jane and Jill in the kitchen. They hurried down to the stables.

"In the big barn in five minutes," Peter told them, and all was hurry and bustle in the wide corridor in front of the boxes, as ponies were saddled and bridled, and last-minute brushings given to their manes and tails. Peter was ready first, and the others arrived in the barn to see him standing at the far end, with his horse at his side. When he saw them coming in, he mounted and sat upright on the impatient Bracken, waiting till they were all in.

Then he rode forward.

"Into line—tallest on my right!" he said, quite loudly. The others got into line with some difficulty. "Keep straight there!" shouted Peter, his voice gaining a little note of authority. "That's better." He looked them up and down, noting with satisfaction the shining flanks, oily hooves and soft manes of the ponies.

"Yes," he said, "not at all bad. Bess's heels aren't quite clean, and Freddy's ears are rough-looking, but it's quite encouraging. Your saddlery looks clean too, but your metal work needs a little more elbow-grease. It ought to really glitter."

Bracken bent his head and mouthed his bit. That certainly shone well. Peter was not a boy to preach what he did not practise.

PETER GIVES A LESSON

"Now turn to your left and circle round me—keep well out!" Pat on Sunny, with his ears back and needing some reminders to keep going, led the little company round. This boring indoor work displeased him, and he felt lazy. Next came Freddy, stepping out gaily, with a light in his eye and a spring in his hooves. Silver behind him kept dancing sideways and lifting her heels slightly at Bess, who was trying to nip.

"Keep order there!" called Peter, noting the floating, silky tails of the ponies and their smooth, shiny quarters. He saw also, with a sort of joyous ache in his heart, those hocks and pasterns rippling in graceful precision. Even in a low-bred mare like Bess, the symmetry of her action was perfect.

When Peter's cavalry had trotted and cantered, and passed their inspection, Peter rode over to the door.

" It's still raining," he reported. " Let's do a little jumping." Pat dismounted and laid their jumping stick across two boxes in the middle of the room, where there were no low beams. The boxes were long, and made quite good wings to the jump. Peter nodded to Pat and, taking a good distance, set Bracken at the jump. Bracken was often difficult over jumps, but Peter knew his tricks, and held him in, concentrating on keeping him straight at the jump.

He was safely over, and Pat followed on Sunny. Sunny refused twice, but Pat got him over the third time, although awkwardly, which made her jag his mouth. Her hands were her chief trouble in riding, for she had ridden too many hard-mouthed ponies, and had yet to learn control with sympathy.

Freddy jumped with his usual ease, Jill swaying slightly to the movement, although she remained in the saddle. All the children jumped forward-seat, but Jill moderated it over low jumps, for Freddy jumped very smoothly and surely.

Silver went over without much trouble, although she would not look at the jump, and Bess went at it with enthusiasm, springing sturdily, with her hocks well under. John had a light seat and fine hands. When he jumped, he hardly seemed to move, so closely did he follow the pony's movements. His only trouble was his short legs, which could not encircle bigger animals.

.   .   .   .

After lunch, when they had all helped to clear it up, the weather had improved, and they decided to ride.

The weak sunshine lit up the wet grass and the pools of

rain-water at the side of the road. Gaps in the clouds disclosed ragged streaks of blue, and nature began to sparkle, decked with glittering rain-drops, which quivered on the fresh leaves in the woods.

Jill breathed the clear air deeply, and wondered at the changed landscape. They trotted down the road which led to the village, and met some children carrying sticks and satchels. The eldest, a dark child with blue eyes, smiled shyly and murmured a broad Devon greeting.

Peter answered her, and the children passed, admiring the mounts, and without the usual fear of village children for ponies.

" I wonder where they come from," said Pat. " I haven't seen them in our village yet."

" They're here on holiday, I expect," said Jill. " They do look nice."

But with that the strangers left their minds, and they filed through a gateway, and having shut the gate behind them, galloped over the field.

Being a low-lying field, it had gathered the water in shallow pools, and the ponies' hooves showered the riders with muddy drops. They had to pull up at the other end, for the hedge was thick and in good repair. Peter opened the gate and held it for them. Then they raced up the slope of the next pasture. The gate was open to the moor, and they galloped through, the ponies shaking their heads with delight in the freedom.

Pat advised them to pull up soon, however, for the moor steepened, and the ponies were blowing. They stopped and turned in their saddles. Below them a farm glowed in the sun, and farther up the valley the village huddled on either side of the stream. It had only some twenty houses; still, it was the centre of that little world, and provided all the wants of farmers for some miles round. It had a small church, by the side of which stood the grey stone vicarage, backed by ragged, untrimmed cedars.

Above them the moors rose, and the slopes on which they stood led the eye upwards to a granite-topped tor which hung in the sky, companioned by the next tors which showed each side of it. Between the three tors narrow saddle-backs intervened, rugged and covered with heather and bracken and stunted gorse.

They urged the ponies upwards again, until they were underneath the crown of grey rock. Now they could see, spread out beneath them, vast distances of valleys, difficult to measure in the clear air, and seeming to drop immediately beneath them, although in reality the slopes were quite gentle and very even.

Peter dismounted and tied Bracken's reins to a clump of heather. The others followed suit, and they all climbed up the rocks, John much ahead of the others, and stood on the highest point, surveying the landscape like conquerors entering a new land. Jane began to feel giddy, and backed away slightly from the edge. John wheeled round and jumped down the rocks, then raced along the ridge to the next tor. Pat followed, and Jane climbed down to see that the horses were still safe.

" What d'you think of Dartmoor?" asked Peter, glancing at Jill.

" It's—awf'ly big," said Jill, not finding words to express herself. " I think it's super."

" Yes, so do I, it's my favourite part of England. We've come here every holiday since last summer. I still don't really know it as Pat does. She's always lived here."

" Lucky thing!" said Jill, and laughing, turned round to climb down again.

"Wait a minute, Jill," said Peter. "I suppose Pat's not been friendly to you. Well, it's because she thought you'd spoil our holiday. I just want to say that Jane and I think you're a jolly good sport, and we like you very much. John always follows Pat, and doesn't mean what he says, but if Pat's ever beastly to you, Jane and I'll always stick up for you, so you needn't worry about her. Mrs. Hever's jolly decent, and I think she likes you; I can't imagine why Pat's often so unfriendly to people. She's very nice when you know her."

"That's awfully nice of you, Peter, thanks," said Jill, smiling at him. She had felt at times friendless and unhappy after Pat's remarks, and Peter's assurance was very comforting, and made her swallow once or twice, with feeling.

. . . .

As the five children rode home, Jill's heart filled with friendliness and happiness. Freddy, though tired, felt the new power in Jill's fingers on the reins, and pranced in front of the other ponies, like a general's horse returning victorious.

Peter noted Jill's happiness, and was glad he had spoken. Pat's rudeness had worried him, though he understood it, and now at last the air was cleared.

That evening Jane started the first of her horse-portraits. She had been making several pencil-sketches of Sunny, and now she traced the outlines of the painting in pencil, filling in, where Sunny moved his position, from her sketches. The others watched her, and in the evening, while she finished it off in paint, they played their racing game, and waited for its perfection.

CHAPTER VIII

The Races—and a Friend

The morning of August 14th was fine and misty, and the children got up in great excitement. They had decided that the big car could not hold the whole party, and Mr. Hever had arranged that Pat and John should travel to the race-meeting with their neighbours, the Martins. So Pat and John had to ride over to the Martins' place before the others started out.

At 11 o'clock, therefore, they set out at a trot on Sunny and Bess. Peter and Jane and Jill watched them go, and then applied themselves to the task of cleaning the car. Soon Mrs. Hever came out to them with a picnic basket, and put it inside the car.

" We shan't be long now," she said.

" How's your arm to-day?" asked Peter.

" Oh, it's getting on all right. It doesn't ache at all now." Mrs. Hever swung the plastered arm and grinned. Then she went to the door and called in: " Hurry up, dear; and could you bring my coat?"

Mr. Hever appeared shortly, smartly clad in breeches and riding jacket, with a tweed cap.

" I hope to pick up a young hunter to-day," he said. " Brown's entering a very nice young four-year-old for the selling hurdle this afternoon, and I ought to get it quite cheap. I shall make a good hunter out of it later." Having astonished all ears with this remark, Mr. Hever helped his wife into the car and got in himself, while the other three piled in at the back. They were all excited at the thought of a new horse, and wondered what it would be like to ride an ex-racer. As the car skidded round corners and crawled past other cars in the narrow Devon lanes, Jill gradually grew accustomed to the dangers of driving in Devon, and enjoyed the narrow escapes as did the others.

Peter looked out of the window and thought of the joys to come. Jane and Jill chatted of the ponies and the country-side which they passed, and also thought eagerly of the day's events. Jill had never been to a race-meeting before, and felt curious, although she thought she knew what it would be like.

As they neared the racecourse, the air seemed to be full of anticipation, and the noises of shouting and horses snorting and whinnying became clearer, until the car swung round into a gateway and began to bump into the field. This field lay next to the racecourse, and was thronged with a variety of people, all hurrying in different directions, and all taken up with their own affairs. Many turned round as a horse came through a gangway cleared for it, some because they knew the horse or the rider, some because they wished to buy it or bet on it, and a few because they loved horses.

Mr. Hever parked the car quite near the finish, in the middle of a long line of shiny, dazzling monsters which the horses suspected of evil designs, especially when the sun reflected on the windows.

In a few minutes they were joined by Pat and John, who had sighted them as they came in the gate, and, having thanked the Martins hastily, came rushing over.

Mr. Hever bought two programmes, which were eagerly scanned. There were six races, three hurdle races and three steeplechases. The first race was over 2 miles, a hurdle race, and was the race for which Mr. Hever's future four-year-old was entered. Then came a three-mile steeplechase, the best race of the day. After that were two unimportant hurdle races, both over $1\frac{1}{2}$ miles, and then two more steeplechases, over 2 and $2\frac{1}{2}$ miles. The Hevers knew several of the entries in each race quite well, and had strong opinions on which would win.

The whole party soon grouped themselves in and about the car, and started an excellent picnic lunch. Pat was highly praised by all for her forethought, as she had seen to the packing of the basket. Mrs. Hever said that everyone had been most helpful, and that she was very pleased with them. After lunch, about half-past one, the five children went round to where the horse-boxes stood, and revelled in the beautiful animals there, some tied to the hedge, others to the boxes, and others again held by miniature stable lads, who chewed straws and slouched in polo-neck jerseys and breeches.

The horses were fine creatures, and in beautiful condition. Most of them were friendly and inquisitive, but a few threw back angry glares from white-rimmed eyes, and laid their ears back ominously. These the children gave a wide berth. The races were due to start at two o'clock, and Peter made sure that they got to the collecting ring by ten minutes to. They waited here for a few minutes, watching the entries and choosing their favourites, and then struggled back through the crowd to their car.

Peter liked a bold chestnut with a star, while Jane and Pat preferred the brown gelding which Mr. Hever had his eye on. John liked a grey mare, and Jill a bay gelding of gentle temperament and long, straight legs.

The horses had to complete almost three circuits of the

course, which was only about $\frac{3}{4}$ mile round. Peter and John bagged the roof of the car, but Jill managed to squash on at the back, and those three gave commentaries on the race to the four below. Mr. Hever followed the caps of the riders, which showed above the crowd, with his glasses, and the horses flashed past them twice in this way. The third time round everyone's neck was craned, and the roar of excited chatter grew, and then suddenly dropped as the brown passed the post first. Jill's bay got in next, and then all the others in a bunch. John's grey had lost its rider, and Peter's chestnut had fallen at the last fence, when it was leading.

"Hm," said Mr. Hever to Peter, "your chestnut should have beaten Brown's gelding. He took that last fence a little too fast. Oh well, I'm off to bid for the brown gelding."

Peter wished him luck, and then he and Jane and Jill wandered over to the horse lines again, to see if there was anything to help with. Peter found the chestnut having a small cut washed, and asked the groom all about the horse. Jane and Jill left him to it, and helped to hold a ticklish horse while it was saddled.

After some time, Jane and Jill realized that the horses were making their way to the collecting ring, and the two friends looked round for Peter. He was nowhere in sight, however, so they hurried after the horses, and wriggled through the crowds until they reached the ring. After a few minutes there, they found their way back to the car, and prepared to see the race.

All this time, Peter had been helping to groom the chestnut, and some time before Jane and Jill had left, Peter had offered to take him over to another box on the opposite side of the course. It took him some time to take the animal round, and by the time it was safely placed in the box, the

race was almost due to start, so Peter rushed up between
the horse boxes to where rising ground gave him a better
view, and came out on to a flat heathy expanse, well above
the racecourse. He could see almost all the jumps, one of
which was very close, where the course abutted on the heath.

The horses had to go round a little more than four times,
and Peter picked his favourite as they passed the first time.
He was a fine short-legged black, called Star of Arabia.
His mane and tail were loose, and he wore only a simple
saddle and snaffle bridle, no martingales at all. The
second time round he was still going perfectly, with a fine
loose action.

As the rider put him at the jump the third time round,
however, he lost his stirrups and his balance, came off and
rolled in the mud, luckily into the shelter of the jump, so
that he was unharmed. Star of Arabia, missing the guiding
hands on his light mouth, cantered off over the heath and,
reaching the hedge, turned round to see what was happening.
Several people tried to catch him, but he kept moving away
from them, and refused to be caught.

Peter, using all his persuasive power, sidled up to him
gingerly, murmuring: " Come on now, old fellow. Steady,
Star. Now, stand!" Nervously the horse obeyed, and Peter
reached successfully for his reins. The rider hurried up to
him, and was full of thanks. Peter asked, rather hesitantly:

" Do you think I could ride him back for you?"

" Well, I don't know," answered the little man thoughtfully, inspecting the mud which had plastered itself over him.

" I'm used to thoroughbreds," said Peter.

" Well, he's a good animal," said the rider, smiling at
Peter. " You can't go wrong with him, as long as you treat
his mouth lightly." And he helped Peter up into the saddle,
while Star stood quietly but expectantly.

.. HARMLESS TOSS

The horse began to walk, excitedly and sideways at first, then more quietly as the man soothed him, walking at his head. Peter gripped firmly with his knees, keeping his heels well down in the short stirrups, and swayed gently to the soft movements of the gelding.

"There's a ditch in the middle of this field," said the man as they came through a gap in the hedge. "You can canter him over it, if you like. But don't let him think he's racing, mind!"

Peter, speechless with excitement, noted the position of the ditch, turned Star straight at it, and started him cantering slowly. The animal had an extremely light and comfortable action, and Peter was able to sit right down in the saddle, and give every attention to the guiding of Star.

He increased pace slightly as he neared the jump, and flew over without hesitation, and with plenty to spare. Peter leant over Star's neck as they rose, and at the height of their spring, boy and horse looked like a statue, caught in that moment for all eternity. Then they landed; the horse gathered himself like a cat and cantered on smoothly. Peter gradually turned him round, and then pulled up to wait for the rider, who was panting along behind them, his dried-up little jockey's face lit up with enthusiasm.

" Jolly good!" he said. " He goes well for you, doesn't he?"

" Yes, I think he's wonderful," said Peter, breathless with admiration.

" It's your riding, boy," said the jockey quite sharply. " How old are you?"

" Thirteen years old, sir."

" You ought to be a jockey, though I suppose you're rather young and will grow a lot yet."

" Yes, that's what I'm afraid of. I'm eight stone already. I'm going to train racers and be a jump jockey."

" Good plan. I'm glad to hear it. Pity you can't flat-race, though. Nothing like it! I got too heavy after a few years."

Peter and the jockey walked back to the box together,

leading Star, who had begun to sweat, and talked long of horses and racing and riding, until the jockey, who was called Tim, had to go for the next race. Peter was simply fascinated with his conversation, and always loved to " talk horse ", anyway. During the two hurdle races he went to the nearest part of the course, and watched his friend win the first on a grey, and come in third in the second race on a bay mare.

Star was entered for the last race, and Peter gave him a grooming and a little hay, while the jockey, who had nothing to ride in the fifth race, sat on the edge of the half-open door and discussed Star's pedigree. Then the two, now good friends, went down to the course to watch the fifth race. After that was over, and won by a fine brown gelding who was entered in the next event, they went back to Star, and made sure his legs were sound. Star seemed very full of beans still, and quite fit to run again, so Peter took him down to the collecting ring, while Tim got some of his mud off and tried to look a little neater. Pat and John were at the ringside, and gaped in astonishment as Peter went past, leading the beautiful black around. Jane and Jill arrived at the ring soon, with Mr. and Mrs. Hever, and they were all very surprised to see Peter in such an important position.

Peter explained as much as he could while he was passing them, and promised to tell the rest when he could get over to the car to watch the race. When Tim came down, Peter saddled Star and straightened his saddle-cloth. Then Tim mounted, and shortly all the entries filed on to the race-course and up to the start. Peter, who had rushed through the crowds as soon as Tim had left the ring, and got to the car just as the horses were off, explained about the black, and his chief rival, the brown who had won the last race, and then the race grew too exciting for talk, so they watched in silence.

Peter and Jill were sitting on the car-roof, their legs dangling through the open shutter, and their eyes glued to the line of moving caps which they could see beyond the crowds.

" Only once more round," said Peter as the horses approached and thudded past, nostrils wide and necks flecked with sweat and foam, for the day was extremely hot, and in addition the recent rain was now beginning to dry out of the ground, and the going was slippery.

" Purple cap's in front," said Jill.

" That's the brown," added Peter, and then: " They're three jumps from home now. Purple's still in front, closely followed by Tim, the green cap, with the others about five lengths behind. Purple's still in front; oh, come on, Tim! Only one more jump. There's a third horse coming up to them. They're over the jump, Purple's still in front. No! It's Tim, it's Tim coming in first! The Purple's dropped back, he's tiring rapidly; yes, the other horse, white and black, I think, it's beating purple. Yes, it's Tim, white and black, and purple."

After that stirring commentary, Peter took his party over to meet and congratulate Tim and Star, who was being led in by a proud and happy owner, who happened to be a friend of the Hevers.

CHAPTER IX

The Hideout is Made

In the evening, after they had returned from the races, Peter and Jill planned to continue Prince's training. They conversed in low tones while the other three were busy with Sunny's portrait, Jane putting the finishing touches and the other two admiring.

"Let's get up really early," said Peter, "about six o'clock, before the others are awake. We can give him an hour then."

"Okay," said Jill, "but how shall we wake up? I'm awfully tired."

"Yes, same here. I'm stiff. But I expect I can use Jane's alarm clock."

"I say, you two," said John, startling them with his sudden appearance, "come and see Jane's picture. It's awfully good." Peter and Jill, hoping he had not overheard, went over to look.

It certainly was good. The chestnut pony was shown in a paddock, against a background of trees, with his head slightly turned towards the artist. He looked a very fine pony, and the picture showed Sunny at his best.

"I'll do Freddy next," said Jane, and Jill wished in her heart that it could be Prince.

"We must find some old picture frames," said Pat. "Then we can hang them round our camp. Let's go now."

So they all followed Pat up to the attic, where such

things were kept with other old junk. They managed to find two of a suitable size, but no more. John offered to make some, but was promptly squashed by Peter.

"We'll buy some," the latter added, "they aren't expensive, second-hand."

. . . .

The first thing that Jill heard the next morning was Peter tapping on the door.

"Hurry up," he said, quite distinctly, but as quietly as possible.

"All right," Jill groaned, rubbing her eyes, which hurt in the light. It was another fine day, and she soon jumped up and got dressed, for she had remembered their plans. When she looked out of the window, she could not see Prince, for most of his field was out of sight behind the stable roof.

A few minutes later she and Peter crept out of the house and ran down to the stables. Here they got Freddy's saddle and bridle, as well as all Prince's breaking-tackle, for Peter wanted Jill to lead Prince from another horse, so that he should know her when level with his back.

Once in the pony's field, they quickly saddled Freddy and haltered Prince. Then they led the pair to a field down by the river, hidden from the house. Although muddy, it was quite flat.

Jill and Peter began Prince's training assiduously, and found him very willing to learn. He accepted the bit in his mouth and the saddle on his back, and stood waiting for his next command. Jill fondled his head, and fed him carrots and sugar, but when Peter came too near the saddle, Prince laid back his ears and tossed up his head, nearly knocking Jill over.

She held on to the reins tightly and soothed him down. Then they began leading him round and backing him, and

JILL SOOTHES THE PUPIL

he seemed quite good at it, so Jill mounted Freddy, and led Prince after her as she trotted and cantered and walked.

"I say," called Peter after some time, "it must be getting late. We'd better stop soon."

"Well, let's just try leaning on his back," said Jill, dismounting. She left Freddy to graze, for he never wandered far. Peter tried to lean on the saddle first, but Prince objected, so they tried it with Peter holding him and Jill leaning on the saddle. Prince was suspicious at first, but he soon grew used to Jill, and took no notice of her weight against his side and on his spine. She removed the saddle and stroked his back firmly until he stood quiet. Then Peter said impatiently:

" Oh, do come on. The others'll be coming down soon. We've got to get everything back in place again before they arrive."

So Jill quickly buckled the saddle round Prince again, and hurried him up to his field, while Peter rode Freddy behind. When they got into the field, they stripped the things off the ponies quickly, and prepared to take them back to the harness room.

Suddenly, however, they heard voices, and then footsteps coming down the path.

" Quick," said Peter, " throw them behind that bush," and they threw the tack out of sight. Peter suddenly realized that the others were carrying halters, and told Jill to get the halter and Freddy's bridle. Jill dived behind, and emerged with the tack as the others came through the gate.

" We're going to ride before breakfast," said Jane, before going up to Silver.

" Yippee!" screamed John, and ran up to the unmoved and equable Bess.

" Don't frighten them, John," said Peter as he went to catch Bracken, who had laid his ears back at John's scream. Jill rebridled Freddy, and mounted him bareback from the gate. They all decided to ride bareback, and filed off in the direction of the valley woods. Jill was thinking of Prince, however, and Peter of Star, neither of them of the ponies which they were riding.

. . . .

Peter and Jill were rather unnerved by their narrow escape, and decided to find some other time to train Prince. The same afternoon, Jane suggested a long picnic ride to explore the woods which had taken John's fancy in the morning.

The sun was very hot, so Peter suggested wearing Arab

headdress, and helped Pat to find strings of beads and old pieces of sheet. Meanwhile Jane and Jill packed up the picnic things, and laid the table for Mr. and Mrs. Hever, so that they would only need to boil a kettle when they wanted tea.

Each of the picnic party took a share of the things, which were carried in knapsacks on their backs. Then they mounted and set off at a walking pace in the direction of the woods.

They cantered along a shady path some way into the woods, and then dropped into a walk as Peter, who was leading, took a narrower turning. Soon the branches grew so low that everyone dismounted. Pat led Sunny a few paces behind Peter and Bracken, and behind her walked Jill with Freddy. Silver was causing trouble, and John was helping Jane to lead her, while Bess followed almost of her own accord.

Suddenly the path grew wider again, and a small stream with steep banks ran alongside it. The children remounted and trotted slowly, still in single file. Peter realized that they were almost on the farther side of the woods, for the ground was rising pretty steeply. After a few minutes they did indeed trot out into bright sunshine, coming through a leafy exit.

"What a super place!" said John. "We haven't ever been here before."

They looked around them. The confines of the woods were very irregular, with many bends and dips, and the moors swept up very abruptly, making the spaces in front of the outer trees concealed and secret.

"Let's ride along the edge of the woods until we find something," said Peter, and led the way.

They stopped every now and again to examine trees which would be good to climb.

"Oh, let's have tea now," said John. "I'm starving."

So they all sat down under a beech, and having secured their ponies to bushes within reach of grazing, they began to eat and talk.

After tea they left the horses to rest for a little while, and wandered along by the woods. Some way farther on, the edge of the woods turned sharply, and in the angle formed was a flat space almost completely surrounded by trees.

"Gosh, it's super!" called John, who had run on ahead. "There's lots of good trees to climb." The other four ran up quickly, and inspected the clearing minutely.

"Jolly good for a camp," said Peter, noting a thick clump of birches in the angle, which was pretty clearly defined.

"Well, then, let's make a camp!" Jane had one of her bright ideas. "Let's have an Arab hideout here."

"Oh yes," agreed Jill eagerly.

Peter and Pat also agreed, and John was simply speechless with delight. Peter had, as usual, yards of variously assorted string in his pocket, and they used that to mark out where the walls of their hut should be. They tied the string to the trees which were at the four corners of the hut. Then Peter led his Arabs into the woods, and they collected as many fallen branches as they could carry.

For about an hour they all worked hard, and at the end of that they had made a small hut, roofed with bracken and heather on a frame, and also a sort of corral by the side of the hut. Peter rolled some logs inside, and put them round the walls as chairs. There was almost enough room to stand up, but only John was short enough to stand straight.

"I say," said Jane, "what about the horses?"

"Oh, gosh!" Peter had forgotten them. "I'll go back for them, if John'll come too."

But in the end everyone went, and when they had remounted, they had a fine gallop back to the hideout. There was not enough room in the corral for all five horses, so they were tied to the outside of the fence while the children built another corral. All this took time, and by the time all the ponies were stowed in one or other of the corrals, the sun was getting low, and Pat advised a speedy return home; so they set off as quickly as possible, having bid their hideout a fond farewell.

.   .   .   .

The same evening Peter made a beautifully neat map, showing the path through the woods and the hideout itself. He marked such tors as came on to his sheet of paper, and also the stream as nearly as possible. There was a good space left, beyond the hideout, to put in new discoveries in that territory.

" Where are the dangerous tribes?" asked John.

" Oh, the enemies. Over to the south, I should think," said Peter.

" Let's spend all our time at the hideout," Pat suggested.

Everyone agreed to that, and mighty plans were made to improve the place: new huts were to be built, and more corrals, proper brush jumps were to be made and set up like a racecourse, on the flatter parts of the moor slopes.

Peter grew quite obsessed by the idea of a racecourse, and laid plans to make a proper one, with white posts and a double course, one for jumps and one for flat. Time soon passed in the planning, and the children had to go to bed.

The next day the children spent the morning looking out more string and rope, also hammer and nails, and Peter even got hold of some planks. Pat said that they ought to find the nearest point in the stream, and have a bathing-pool there.

"Good idea," said Peter. "Look, don't you think everyone ought to have some definite part of the building operations to do? For instance, I'll take over the racecourse, and Pat can do one hut, Jill another. John, you can do the bathing-pool, when we've all prospected and found the best place."

"Well, I suppose we could, but won't the work take longer that way? We ought to get the actual hideout ready, then the racecourse, then the bathing-pool. Then we can use what we've already made while we're making the rest." Jane was never afraid to combat her brother's ideas.

"Let's try both ways," said Pat, and Jill agreed, fearing a split in the party. John was not interested, and said nothing. He did not mind *how* they did it, but what they did.

"The first day we'd better work together," said Jill, "because of finding the bathing-pool and marking the race-course. We can just mark them out, not working on them, and then we can get on with the huts."

So that is what they did that afternoon. The sun was still very bright and hot, and after leaving the ponies un-saddled in the corrals, the children gladly plunged into the cool woods in search of the stream. They found it, after some time, and searched along it. There were no very deep pools, but at one widely cut bend the stream broadened out for a few yards, and Peter suggested damming the stream where the banks closed in again, and then scooping out as much river-bed as possible.

Then the children found a rather quicker way back to the hideout, and began to mark out a racecourse. They did it with string and short stakes. The course was a wide oval, possibly half a mile round. There was one sharp turn in it, which could constitute start and finish if necessary. The steepest slope on it Peter had planned to be taken uphill. The course was right-handed.

Peter went up to the nearby tor to look on the race-course from above. The others were too hot to bother, and were not so keen on the course, anyway.

After all this hard work they felt hungry, and tucked into the basket of food like demons. When that was all demolished, they rested for a little while. Peter was planning several races which they could run; Jill was wondering when they could train Prince; John was wishing for some help with the bathing-pool; Pat was feeling very happy and lazy, and thinking of her pony, Sunny; and Jane was very busy sketching Freddy, and getting several poses as he moved about.

CHAPTER X

Triumph—and Trouble

The next day, at breakfast, Mr. Hever startled everyone into excitement by saying:

" The brown gelding is coming in this afternoon. You can help clear out a box for him, Pat."

" Oh, good!" said Pat, her eyes sparkling. " When's he coming?"

" Oh, any time from two to four." Mr. Hever buried himself in *The Times*, while everyone else chattered, for a few minutes, and then added: " I want some things from the saddler, and I really need some more bran. Would one of you go? I've got to go over and travel back with the gelding. Brown says he's my responsibility on the journey."

Peter promised to send someone, and took down a list of the things to be got, and to be done. After washing up, the children all met in the barn and decided who was to go to the village. They decided that Pat knew the villagers best, and John was always ready for something out of the ordinary run of things, so they let him go with Pat. Mr. Hever came in at that point, and asked them to take Doricles and Sandra to the forge.

About quarter of an hour later, therefore, Pat and John set off, each leading another horse, and expecting to spend the whole morning in the village, for their own ponies' shoes were wearing thin, and needed an inspection.

Peter, with an eye to training Prince, asked Jane to sweep

out the spare loose-box while he and Jill trotted Firefly
and Ben round the field for a little. Actually, he knew that
Ben needed little exercise, and he had planned to let Jill
carry on with Prince's training while he rode Firefly and
led Ben. So that was what they did.

" How long do you think we can carry on?" asked Jill.

" Well, Mr. Hever's leaving in about a quarter of an
hour," answered Peter, " so we can start then. Jane will
have to spend about an hour altogether, so we can have
about half an hour with safety. You can ride Ben round at
first."

" Shall we go in the field by the river again?" asked Jill.
Peter nodded.

" Yes, it's a good way from the house, and out of sight,"
he said. So they collected the three bridles and Prince's
saddle, and ran down the path to the horses' field. They
bridled Firefly and Ben, and left Prince's tack behind a
bush. Then Peter gave Jill a leg up on to Ben, and heaved
himself on to Firefly.

They trotted and walked round and round the field; the
horses being quite well-behaved, they could talk to each other,
and they found much to say on the subjects of school, careers,
riding and racing. After about ten minutes, Mr. Hever came
up and gave Peter last-minute directions as to the clearing
of the stables, and then went off to get into his car and drive
over to Brown's.

Jill rode Ben up to Prince's field, and put the reins
round his neck to lead him back. He came easily, and Jill
did not have to dismount from Ben.

After that, for a long time Jill led Prince round and
round, made him back and passage, and gave him a lengthy
test of all he was supposed to have learnt.

" Jill," called Peter, after perhaps half an hour, " get

up on to Ben, and lead Prince beside you!" Peter had to dismount to help Jill up again, but then the three horses were set to cantering round the field, with Prince in between the other two, and Jill and Peter each holding one rein. He objected at first, but soon grew used to it, and even submitted to Peter's leg being thrown across his saddle as they cantered.

"Gosh, he's much quieter!" said Peter as they pulled up. "You'll soon be able to mount him."

"Oh, do you really think so?" asked Jill, her eyes alight with joy.

"Yes, I do," said Peter. "I say, though, it must be time to get him back again. Jane may come down any minute." But just as they were taking him towards the gate, still between the bigger horses, Jane came down the path and saw them.

"Whatever—!" she stammered, eyes and mouth wide. "Peter, what are you doing? I hope you haven't hurt him?"

"No, quite the contrary. Come and watch. Jill, canter him round again." Jill did so dutifully, loving the fiery little black, and Peter's eyes lit with triumph as Prince responded perfectly to Jill's commands.

"Gosh, how wonderful!" said Jane; "he even responds to words!"

. . . .

Jane had to be let into the whole secret, and Jill explained their plans while the two girls were cooking lunch. Peter put the saddle and bridles away and cleaned some tack, and then came into the kitchen to help Jill persuade Jane over to their ambitions and way of thinking. Jane at first was horrified at the liberty of training someone else's horse, but the other two gradually argued her round.

"And you see how much better Prince is. You see, he trusts Jill." Peter concluded his oration on the subject, and just at that moment Mrs. Hever came in.

"Come along, you surely aren't quarrelling?" she said, laughing.

"Oh no," said Jane, but the three children had difficulty in hiding their surprise.

That afternoon everyone hung around the stables and near the gate, waiting to see the new stable inmate, whom they wanted to call " Jigger ". He had of course a proper Stud Book name, but that was too long. At about 3.30 o'clock the horse box rattled slowly up the road, drawn by Mr. Hever's own car.

Peter went up to help the stable lad get the horse out, and then led him round the stable yard, to let the animal shake his cramped legs. Everyone stood round admiring, but Jill was thinking of Prince, and wondered how soon she could ride him.

Peter then led Jigger into the loose-box, and settled him with hay and a small ration of corn for the night. Then Mr. Hever had to drive the stable lad back, and the rest of the household had tea.

After tea, while Pat tried out the brown gelding, under Mrs. Hever's guidance, Peter and Jane and Jill discussed Prince in low tones.

"I thought she'd heard us this morning," whispered Jane.

"Well, perhaps she did, and is saying nothing," Jill suggested.

"Oh no, surely she'd say something," said Peter. " We must train him to-morrow morning, if possible."

"Oh, good, I'm longing to see Jill with him," said Jane.

As it happened, they got a chance to work with him

that evening, because a friend rang up and invited Mr.
and Mrs. Hever to a housewarming, and included Pat as
company for her two children. When she heard that Mrs.
Hever had the other four with her, she invited them too,
but Mrs. Hever explained the lack of room in the car.

" I'll take two of you," she said, turning to her family.
" It had better be John and—Jill, I think."

" Oh no," said Jill, seeing Pat's ill-concealed disappointment. " I think Pat ought to go, she was invited first of
all."

" Well, then, you go instead of me," said John, not
really too keen on the idea, but heroically being gallant.

" No, John, you'll enjoy yourself. After all, you're the
youngest."

" Well, Jill, if you're really sure—it's very nice of you.
You three don't mind being left?" Mrs. Hever asked them.

" No, of course not," said Peter.

And indeed, as soon as the other four had departed,
after washing and changing, Peter, Jane and Jill danced
round the sitting-room in glee.

" Rotten old housewarming!" yelled Peter, rushing
out of the french window.

" The house all to ourselves!" screamed Jane, following
him.

" And Prince ready to be trained!" shouted Jill as they
ran across the lawn.

They ran down to the stables, got three bridles for their
ponies, and Prince's saddle and bridle as well. Then they
were off down through the fields and into the ponies' field
in a few moments. They caught Bracken, Silver and Freddy,
and bridled them. Peter showed Jill how to jump on to the
pony without a saddle, and then got up on Bracken in the
same way. Jane was already up, and so Jill walked Freddy

wards Prince and called him. He came up, and Jill bridled
im, after dismounting from Freddy again. Then Peter
addled Prince, surprisingly enough without any trouble,
nd all four ponies were then circled round the field, Jill
ading Prince.

The Arab behaved admirably, and afterwards did all his
acking and other tests perfectly.

"It's wonderful," said Jane, "but I wonder what'll
appen when you try to mount him."

"Nothing, I believe," said Peter. "Jill, do you feel like
nounting him now? I think he'll let you to-day."

"All right," said Jill quietly, hiding the sudden joy and
rror in her heart.

She slipped off Freddy, and gave the reins to Jane.
eter did likewise with Bracken, and held Prince's head.
ll this was done in silence, and now he said:

"Talk quietly to him, Jill, so that it seems quite
rdinary."

Peter's lips were pressed tightly together as Jill put her
ot in the stirrup. She talked quietly, soothing Prince's
ar, and Peter stroked the animal's neck.

Jill swung up, and sat perfectly still in the saddle.
rince threw his head up and flickered his ears back. Then
o one moved for some seconds, and Peter let go the rein.
ll clicked her tongue and pressed her legs on Prince's sides,
rging him forward. He stopped, drew back on his hind
gs, which were spread under him, and pricked his ears
rward. Suddenly he sprang forward and began to gallop.
ll made him go round and round the field, after she had
covered her balance from that first spring, and steadied
im gradually until he was cantering. Meanwhile Peter
nd Jane had been watching, at first in horror, then joy
nd admiration.

Jill gradually slowed him down, and brought him to standstill in front of the others. He was sweating and panting and looked a little nervous, but he stood quietly and arched his neck gently. Jill slipped off him and held his head in her hands. This he submitted to, and also he allowed her t kiss his white star. Soon, however, independence asserted itself, and he tossed his head, his eyes gleaming and softl luminous. His forelock rose in the evening breeze, and h stamped on the ground with a foreleg.

"Jill!" said Peter, and words stuck in his throat. Every one was silent. Jill held the end of Prince's reins, an watched him graze.

"It's wonderful," said Jane, unconsciously repeatin her previous reaction.

"Yes," burst out Peter at last, "I am glad, Jill! Yo can ride him like an old hand, and I think—yes, you ough to be first in command."

"Oh no," said Jill modestly. "Anyway, Pat wouldn like it. Besides, you're a very good leader."

"Oh well, I expect you're right. Are you going to rid him any more to-night?" Jill shook her head. "No," Pete went on, "that's best. Let's go back and rub him dow then hunt up some supper."

And that is what they did. Jill rubbed him down wit great care and quite slowly, while the other two stood b and admired the pony in glowing terms. Then she stoo and watched him with the others. Suddenly the emotio excitement and fatigue swept over Jill, and she burst int tears on the friendly Jane's shoulder.

"What's the matter?" asked Peter, wondering wh sorrow should follow joy.

"Oh, nothing," said Jill, sniffing and grinning agair "I'm so happy!"

" Oh, you women!" exclaimed Peter. " Come along and let's get supper."

.   .   .   .

They had an Arabish sort of supper, seated cross-legged on the floor, and then a long, extremely horsey discussion, which lasted unawares long past their bedtime. Peter drew diagrams of racecourses, wrote schedules of race-cards and gymkhanas, and they all drew foals, cart-horses, stallions and ponies. Jane was the best, of course. Then they realized how late it was and rushed up to bed, just before the others came in.

.   .   .   .

The next afternoon they went up to their hideout. Very early in the misty morning, Peter, Jill and Jane had trained Prince again, and later all five children had done some gymkhana practice for bending and jumping with Mr. Hever, who was trying out Jigger, and finding him a strong ride and a good jumper over show-jumps.

When they reached the hideout, everyone pulled up short and gasped with astonishment. Peter's markings for the racecourse had been pulled up and left in a heap. Worst of all, the huts had been pulled down, the log seats chopped up, and the corral fences pulled to pieces. A note was left on a tree, saying:

" Whoever has been here, look out! This is our tor, and no one may trespass here. If you build here again, and deface our moors, it will mean WAR."

It was signed: " The Moors ".

CHAPTER XI

War!

"Gosh, the rotters!" said John.

"We must have revenge," said the valiant Peter, remembering his Arab character.

"I should jolly well think so!" Pat was very annoyed. All that work! Jane and Jill just sat still in their saddles and surveyed the wreckage.

Soon, however, they dismounted and tied their ponies to trees or stumps and set to work tracking for signs of the enemy.

"No," said Peter, "the note's all they've left. Well, we shall have to wait until they come here again, that's all."

"That's a good idea," said Pat. "Then we can ambush them."

"Yes, or track them to their homes," Jane added, "and then raze them to the ground."

"Oh, don't be an ass!" said Peter. "No, we must study their habits, when we know who they are, and then take them prisoners. I've always wanted some real prisoners."

"Oh yes! Super!" screamed John excitedly, turning a somersault.

"Steady on!" said Peter. "Now look, we'd better have someone up on the tor, under cover, who can give the alarm if they see them coming."

"Yes, we can take it in turns," said Jill.

" Oh, let's have two up there," said Jane, " it's miserable otherwise."

" Okay, if you like."

John and Jane took first turn, and the other three started to rebuild the hut, hoping it was not vain labour.

After about half an hour, Jill went up to relieve John, and she and Jane had a good long chat while they kept watch. Once Jane thought she saw a black shape crossing the valley, but it was only a stray sheep of that unusual colour. It was fun, just sitting there in the sun, talking and watching the other three working down below, and Jane was sorry when Peter came up to relieve her.

" Pat and John are in the middle of roofing the hut," said Peter breathlessly, for the climb was steep. " You'd better help with that, Jane. Gosh," he puffed, flopping down on the grass, " what a hot day! I suppose there's no sign of the enemy?"

" Not a hope," said Jill, leaning back against a rock, watching birds in the sky.

" What on earth's that, then!" Peter sat up suddenly and pointed at the long-suffering scapegoat, the sheep.

" Okay, okay," Jill laughed, " it's only a sheep."

Peter calmed down, and they began to talk about Prince.

" He was much better this morning," Peter remarked, " he didn't pull so much. Is he comfortable to ride?"

" Oh, very comfortable," said Jill; " he's smooth-strided and it's easy to stay on. The only thing is, he throws his head about too much."

" Yes, that's true. But he'll tone down soon. After all, he knew the tests perfectly, and it's only the second ride. You do ride him well."

" Oh, but you're such a good trainer," said the modest Jill; " it's your training that makes him so quick."

" Well, perhaps it's Prince himself," said Peter softly. " He's the best horse I've ever seen."

" Better than Star?"

" Miles."

They were silent, and both had in mind a picture of the beautiful animal in question.

" I bet he'll race well," said Peter suddenly. " I wish we had something to race against him. Nag and Nagina are too old and stately."

" What about Bracken—you said he was pretty fast?"

" Oh no, he's not in the same class! He's fast as ponies go, but Prince is an Arab. I mean, I love Bracken, 'cos he's my own pony, and therefore I think he's marvellous, but in point of fact Prince is streets ahead."

" Oh, gosh!" Jill could find no words, for she felt so proud of Prince.

Just then Pat came up to relieve Jill, and the pleasing discussion had to end. Jill ran down the hill, and put all her energies into building a stout corral. John and Jane were remaking " furniture " for the hut, and as they nailed planks on to logs and fixed shelves to the walls, they talked animatedly of the Horse Show which was to be held at a nearby village in the last part of the holidays. Jill listened as she worked, and stored up as much information about shows as she could, to be able to talk about it to Pat on equal terms.

Meanwhile Pat and Peter were discussing the enemies, and the best way to deal with them. They also arranged plans for a day for their own races.

" I expect Mum would disapprove, so we'd better not mention it. Still, I suppose she'll guess anyway." Pat usually confided everything to her mother, sometimes with unfortunate results.

" Yes, I think she ought to know, really. But I bet she'll forbid it."

" Oh well, we'd better ask the others and think about it."

Peter and Pat went on to discuss their forces, as any good commander and second-in-command should. They had forgotten to use the Arab names lately, and now they had almost forgotten what they had been called.

The book, *Seven Pillars of Wisdom,* had proved too big an obstacle to be read right through, and it had been put away in one of Jill's drawers. Indeed, they were hardly Arabs any more. The only things they kept were the head-dress and several customs they had made up for themselves, like saluting the chief with upraised arm, and sitting round cross-legged for meals.

Soon John came up to take the last watch with Peter, and introduced the subject of the Horse Show, which Peter took up eagerly. They planned which events they would enter for, and hoped secretly to win some of the classes.

Soon the last watch was up, and everyone had a hurried tea before packing up to go home. They had repaired all the damage except to the racecourse, and Peter felt that it must be redesigned, anyway.

The enemy had made no sign, and seemed almost non-existent. Peter wrote a scathing reply to their note, and pinned it up:

" To the Moors! This is our hideout, because we built here first. If you touch it again, you stand in danger of your lives. We're quite ready for war, if you want it! The Arabs."

They stared at it for a minute, then, satisfied, mounted their ponies and set off in the direction of home. But later on three horsemen quietly entered the camp and, having read theirs, pinned up another note, looked round the camp, and then rode away again.

.   .   .   .

That evening the new cook arrived, and proved to be a very good one. Peter asked if they could take out lunch as well as tea the next day.

" Where *do* you go?" asked Mrs. Hever, laughing, for she knew well that it was probably a secret.

" Well, we've got a hideout," began Pat, and then looked at the others.

" Oh, never mind. I always had hideouts too, very secret ones. With your mother, Jill. By the way, I've written your parents and asked them to come here for a few weeks after they get back from the cruise."

" Oh, good!" said Jill. " That's awfully kind of you."

The next morning, the children got up good and early, and hunted round for instruments of war. They could find nothing beyond some ropes and bamboo spears, but that was quite enough to manage on horseback, anyway. Peter and Jill had no time at all to train Prince, and fumed in consequence.

Soon after breakfast they all set out, with bursting knap-sacks, for they would be away for about nine hours, and also with permission to light a fire. The sky was overcast, but otherwise it was a pleasantly mild day. When they reached the hideout, they were very pleased to see it still standing, and eagerly crowded round when they saw the note on the tree.

" To the Arabs," Peter read out. " We much admire your courage in rebuilding at once, and consider you a worthy foe. So let it be War. What rules of war, if any, do we fight under? We are only three, and must get some allies. You are also free to get more, if you can! You can leave

a message on the advertisement board of the village shop.
The Moors."

"Gosh, they're getting down to it quickly!" said Peter.

"Good job too. I hate waiting," growled John, amid
laughter from the others.

Then they settled down to discuss the feud. They decided
very soon on open warfare, and then went on to discuss
ways and means.

"Surprise," said Peter weightily, "is the most important
element in attack."

"Oh, let's get on with it quickly!"

"Well, all right," said Peter, getting down to brass
tacks, "we've got to find out more about them, first. I hope
they're coming here again. Then we must lay an ambush
and trap them."

"Does that mean more waiting up on the tor?"

"Well, it ought to, but perhaps we needn't, because I
want to do the bathing-pool to-day, and there we shall all
be hidden."

So they took the horses well into the woods and tied
them securely, then got on with their bathing-pool. From
time to time Peter sent someone to see if the enemy were
about, but they never were.

The pool was hard work, and the dam was only just
above the water, and kept breaking down again, when they
all downed tools and voted for lunch.

They ate it just inside the edge of the wood, where
they could observe the camp without being seen. After they
had made their way through a good portion of the day's
food, they lay back and rested from their labours.

Suddenly they felt the vibration of hoof-beats in the
ground, and three riders galloped up on shaggy Dartmoor
ponies, one bay and two brown. The children were those

they had met once before, when they were going out on the
moors. Until now they had forgotten them, but on seeing
them again, Peter had remembered their strong, resolute
air and fearless glances. The eldest, a girl, obviously the
leader, rode the bay, and the other two, who looked like
twin brothers, rode the browns. She looked about twelve,
they about ten or eleven.

They looked around the camp, and saw no change,
except that the note had been taken away. Suddenly Pat
nudged Peter, and pointed to their own ponies' tracks, clearly
leading into the woods. All five of our party held their breath
and hoped. Luckily the tracks were not noticed, and the
enemy sat on logs and talked together.

" I don't know where they've gone, Bill," said the girl.
" I was sure they'd be here now, but there's no sign of them."

" No, that's right, Ann. What do you think, Jack?"

" I don't know. Seems as if they've been frightened
away."

" No! They're too smart for that, Jack. I think they're
probably preparing for war."

" Yes, that'll be it. Perhaps we'd better do the same."

" No, Bill, you know well what our plans are. We've
got to find out when they'll come here, and get here first.
Then we hide in the trees, and spring down on them."
They agreed to this plan, and hiding their saddles and
bridles in the bushes at the other side of the clearing, they
turned the ponies loose.

" That's jolly clever," whispered Peter; " they look like
wild ponies."

Then the three children each chose a different tree, and
scaled it rapidly.

" I hope they don't stay there long," whispered John.
" I'm getting stiff."

WATCHING FOR THE ENEMY

The three newcomers, Ann, Bill and Jack, must have got stiff too, for after about quarter of an hour they all climbed down.

"I'm too stiff to stay there any longer," said Ann, laughing. "I don't suppose they'll come now, anyway."

And all three called their ponies with a shrill whistle, and resaddled them.

"Jolly well trained," whispered Peter. Then the other three mounted and rode off down the valley.

Peter got up. "Who's got the least conspicuous pony?" he asked.

"Jill and I," said John.

"Yes; well, you two must follow them as closely as possible. We'll follow a little way behind you." They all mounted and walked their ponies just inside the outermost line of trees, keeping the three enemies in sight, but not going too close on their heels.

Their direction was down the new branch of the woods, and after a little way those woods ended, and they came into a wide valley between the moors, with a deeply cut river flowing through it. The enemies turned upstream, and began to canter. Peter at once caught up with Jill and John.

"Over to the river-side," he said. Everyone cantered over, luckily unseen, and continued at the same pace between the banks of the river, where a narrow strip of dry river-bed was left. Here they were quite well hidden. Soon their enemies stopped and dismounted at a small old cob-and-thatch cottage. They turned the ponies loose again and went inside. Peter dismounted and tracked round the cottage on hands and knees before leading his cavalry homewards again.

CHAPTER XII

Jill is Lost

Having now found out much about the enemy, the next morning Peter decided to put a message in the village shop-window.

"They must mean the grocer's," said Pat as they polished their bridles before breakfast. "What shall we say in the note?"

"Oh, nothing much. Just: 'War is declared from 12 noon to-day. No rules are being used. We agree to the addition of allies. The Arabs.' That's nice and short." Peter wrote it down on a piece of card as he spoke, signing himself with a flourish.

"Who'll take it?" he asked.

"I will," said Pat, "if you like."

"Oh no," Jill exclaimed, "you're needed at the hide-out. Besides, I've never seen the village properly."

"Gosh, that's jolly nice of you!"

"You'll have to follow us on later. You won't mind coming all that way by yourself?"

"No, of course not. I shall have Freddy for company."

At breakfast Mrs. Hever said that Jill had better get some things from the shop while she was there, and so Jill set off with a soft basket over one arm, and the other hand on her reins.

The day promised quite well, but in the west the sky was still grey. The other four children set out for the hide-out a little while after Jill had gone.

She, meanwhile, was trotting along the road to the village. A west wind was blowing, and the air soon began to feel damp. The grey clouds in the west slowly spread over most of the sky and began to deepen in colour.

"Bother!" thought Jill, "it's going to rain again. I expect the others will turn back."

The road began to slope down, and Jill pulled Freddy in to a walk, for the surface was quite slippery with the moisture in the air. The pony's hooves clicked over the bridge which spanned the little stream, and then Jill kicked him into a trot as the first raindrops began to fall. Looking up, Jill realized that a heavy mist was thickening over the moors, and remembered all the grim stories she had heard about Dartmoor fogs, and hoped indeed that her friends had turned homewards.

When she trotted into the village, she left Freddy with his reins looped over some railings, and did the shopping for Mrs. Hever. Then she asked about putting the card in the window.

"Why, yes, midear, uv course yu can. Is it somethin' you're sellin'? Oh no! I see, it's some game you're playin'? Well, well, it's to be war, is it? Well, well. Oh no, dear, never mind about the money, if it's just a game. I've plenty of room on my board. There! Now I've stuck it on where they can't fail to see it. That's right, midear. Stayin' with Mrs. Hever, are ye? Well, well, hurry along back now, for there's going to be a real thick fog."

Jill bade the garrulous old shopkeeper good-day, and went to mount Freddy.

Before heading for home again, she had a look round the village, but it was a short look, for the rain had begun to run down her neck, and she had no mac with her.

She and Freddy trotted along the road at a good speed

and soon reached home. Jill could hardly see their own little tor, and the next ones were completely blotted out in the fog.

"Is that Peter?" asked Mrs. Hever from the kitchen as Jill clattered into the yard. "Oh no, it's Jill. I wish the others would come back. I'm afraid they'll get lost."

Jill had dismounted to take the groceries into the kitchen, and then went back to mount Freddy.

"Oh no, Jill, you'd better stay at home. It's no good five getting lost. Peter's got a bit of sense; I expect they'll be all right."

So Jill turned Freddy out into the pony field, not forgetting to give Prince a bit of carrot and some sugar, and then went back to the house. She sat in the kitchen, which was nice and warm, and talked to Betty, the cook, a comfortable, fat woman in middle age, with a rosy, cheerful face. While she chatted about London, Dartmoor, horses and the weather, among other things, she coloured the pencil map Peter had drawn the night before of the hideout and all the country round the house.

About an hour later Mrs. Hever had become quite worried, and as Mr. Hever was out on business, Jill offered to go up to the hideout.

"I can't possibly get lost," she said; "the path is quite clear, and I won't wander on to the moor."

"Well, I am tempted to let you," said Mrs. Hever, looking at the clock. It said 11.30. "All right, then, you can go. But do be careful."

Jill raced down to the field and caught Freddy. Suddenly she wondered where Prince was, for he had not come up to her as he usually did. She trotted round the field, which was half hidden in mist, and discovered that he was gone. She rode up to the house again at full speed, and threw herself off Freddy at the back door.

8   (G 391)

" Prince isn't in his field!" she exclaimed, out of breath. " He must have been stolen!"

" Oh no, surely not. . . . He might have run away. I hope he hasn't, it's a bad sign. Anyway, he'll be all right, I'm sure. You'd better get off."

Jill saddled Freddy and hurried him down the road. He disliked the mist, and kept hesitating, so Jill gave him a few reminders with a stick she had pulled out of the hedge. Then they cantered through the wood, jumping in their stride the few logs which lay across the path. Then, out of the wood on the other side, Jill was careful to keep close to the trees. Freddy was blowing, so they dropped to a walk. All that was visible were the wet, dripping trees, rising out of sight into the mist.

.   .   .   .

Meanwhile, Peter and his Arabs had arrived at the hide-out, and started on the rebuilding work, which now consisted of the new racecourse, a second hut, and a third corral, and also a lot more excavating work on the dam. Peter decided to plan out the racecourse on the ground, and then to make as accurate a diagram as possible, on which to work out the details. After that, he suggested finishing off the bathing-pool. The sky was still quite blue as they mapped out the course, and they did not realize how misty it was getting until they had done all they could to the bathing-pool, and come out into the clearing again.

" I say," said Peter, " Jill's being a jolly long time." Then he saw that even the nearest tors were blotted out, and that the moving mist was reducing visibility rapidly.

" Gosh!" said Jane nervously, " do you think she's come out and got lost in this?"

" How could she?" asked Pat.

" Oh, *she* could easily," groaned John, making a face.

USEFUL PRACTICE

"John, don't be horrid," said Jane.

"Anyway, it wouldn't be hard to get lost in this." Peter considered, and added: " She could take the wrong turning in the wood, or even wander on to the moors after leaving the wood. I think Pat and I will go out to look for her. No, you can't come, John! Someone's got to be here in case she comes. We'll be back soon."

And so they walked out of the camp, in the direction of the nearest tor. John and Jane sat down to wait.

Just a few minutes later, Jill trotted into the camp and slid off Freddy.

"Mrs. Hever's very worried about you all," she said quickly; "she kept me in for a bit. Then she let me come and look for you. Why, where are Pat and Peter?"

"They've just gone out looking for you," said John. "We thought you'd got lost coming here."

"Oh dear. Well, never mind, I'll wait here for them till they come back. You two had better get back as quickly as possible, to calm Mrs. Hever down."

The two younger children mounted their ponies, and Jane promised to return with some food and to keep Jill company.

And then Jill was left alone in the cold, misty camp, but she was cheered to see the three ponies, Freddy, Sunny and Bracken. Then Peter had left a hammer and nails on the bench he had made, and that was nice and ordinary. Still, Jill shivered.

After some time, she imagined she heard a voice, calling her name, and the second time she heard it, she recognized it was Peter's.

"I wonder if he's all right," she thought. "Well, I'll follow the voice. I can't get lost that way." So she hurried over the damp and slippery turf towards it. Then she heard it again, in a different place, and changed her direction. She stopped and called out. No one answered, and she turned round to go back again.

But she did not find the camp.

"Oh," she thought, with panic, "I'm lost! What can I do?" She tried to think it out, and came to the conclusion she ought to go to her right. Something was wrong, however, for the ground was rising. Jill turned to her left, and walked along on the side of the moor.

"This is wrong," she thought, but felt less panicky. Soon, however, the ground dropped again, and she walked on quickly. "This must come to the woods again soon," she thought.

But it did not, for soon Jill came to a stream, deeply cut into the valley.

"Oh, this is the Moors' stream," she thought, feeling happier. "But are the woods below or above me?"

She decided this time to sit down and wait for the fog to lift, and wished she had done so before. She felt very tired with her fear and her exertions, for she had run some of the way in her more panicky moments.

"I'm lucky not to have hit a bog," she said to herself. "I don't know them to look at, 'specially on a day like this." She sat down on a tree stump, and pulled her coat collar closer round her neck. She wondered where Prince was, and then where she was, and after that, how much longer the fog would last. "Well," she argued in her mind, "if I were downstream, I'd have had to cross close to the woods, because they grow close to the river, so I must be upstream from them. And these fogs sometimes last for days, I've heard. I'd better follow the stream until I see the woods by the river." So she began to walk downstream, following the narrow ledge of dry river-bed. She went on for some way, until a stronger wind blew up, and the mist began to lift.

Jill thankfully decided to sit down and wait for the mist to clear. But what a scene greeted her eyes when it did clear! The hills and tors were quite strange, and the woods were on the wrong side of the stream!

"Oh, golly," she thought, "what have I done now?" She waited a little longer, and as the mist was nearly gone, she decided to climb a nearby tor, to see the country and find her own range of moors. She set off to climb the tor.

. . . .

Meanwhile Peter and Pat had walked back into the camp to find no one there but the ponies.

"That's funny," said Peter. "I heard her voice a little while ago. I suppose Jane and John have taken her to see the pool."

"But their ponies are gone, and Jill's isn't."

"I know. Well, we'd better wait."

They sat down and waited, and a few minutes later Jane returned with a tin of sandwiches. She explained what she knew, and Peter began to realize what had happened to Jill. They decided to wait there for her, after having called her in vain, and see if they could find her when the mist cleared.

"It ought to clear soon," said Pat, knowing the weather signs.

"I should think she's sitting down too, waiting for it to clear," said Peter cheerfully.

"I do hope so," said Jane unhappily.

When the mist did at last begin to clear, Peter went up to the tor and looked round. He saw no one, however, and went down again.

"Perhaps she's at home already," suggested Pat.

" Yes, she may be. Look, I think we'd better go back. If she isn't there, we must send out a search party."

So they set off and took Freddy with them, because he could not be left.

. . . .

Jill, once she had reached the top of her tor, began to recognize the country. She saw the woods, which she had passed and missed in the fog. She saw that she must work her way back along the north side, and began to climb down the tor, for it was some way to go. She walked for about a quarter of an hour, and then was most surprised to hear a whinny.

Suddenly a black shape galloped up to her, and she saw that it was Prince. How glad she felt! She decided to mount him and hope that he would take her home again. She made a very rickety halter out of the string in her pocket, and then set off on the pony. He did get her back safely, and when she dismounted near the house, kept rubbing his head against her arm.

As they walked into the stable yard, Mrs. Hever rushed out to meet them, followed by the other children.

CHAPTER XIII

The War is Ended

" There you are!" said Mrs. Hever, relief and joy evident on her face. " Why, you've got Prince with you as well. What's been happening to you, and where did you find him? But never mind that for the moment. Pat, you take Prince and rub him down, and give him some mash. Jill, come along indoors and get dry. You can tell us then."

Jill obeyed, and went inside to have a hot bath and change into pyjamas and dressing-gown. Then she sat by a warm fire and drank cocoa, while she told the others about her eventful day. Jill was surprised to find that it had been four o'clock when she came in.

" It was lucky you were no later," said Peter; " we were just sending out a search party of villagers."

" Gosh," said Jill, " how exciting!"

" But how on earth did you manage to get Prince and lead him home?" asked Pat, who had wondered very much at this feat, and also at some muddy marks on Prince's sides, which could well have been heel-marks.

" Oh, he came up to me, and then it was easy to halter him. I expect he was fed up with being out in the wet."

" But he could have gone home without you. You said he led you home."

" Well, yes, he did know the way more than I did. I don't know why he came up to me. He often does in the field." Jill looked at Peter for help.

Peter stepped into the breach and said: "Well, the horse trusts her because she likes the horse. It often happens that way, doesn't it, Mrs. Hever?"

"Yes, I believe so," she answered. "Well, I must get some tea. Cook says she's too shaken up to do anything, but I think it's laziness, personally."

As soon as Mrs. Hever's footsteps had safely died away, Peter began to discuss the war in general and, in particular, how to capture the enemies.

"Their house is situated on the opposite side of the moors, and the shortest way round is via the hideout." Peter considered the map which he had just received from Jill, the one which she had coloured in the morning. "The best place for an ambush would be where the woods end at the stream. We can watch their house from there, and I think there are some rocks on the lower slopes of the moors. Those slopes are quite steep, so the entrance is quite narrow."

"The entrance to what?" asked Pat.

"Oh, you know what I mean. The entrance to the sort of valley between the Moors and the woods. It's like a valley really."

"Could we put string across to trip the ponies?" asked John bloodthirstily.

"No, we couldn't!" Peter was very firm. "The animals are not to be hurt! Anyway, string would just snap."

"I wonder how many allies they'll get hold of," said Jane thoughtfully.

"Not many with ponies, I should think, and infantry's not much good."

"It can be useful," Peter reminded them, "to carry stores and in tracking."

"Yes, but they can't keep up with a cantering horse," said Pat.

"No, but they can with a walking one, and remain unseen as well."

"We'd better not move about slowly at all, then," said Jill. "And we must keep together, or we'll be captured ourselves."

"How are we going to catch them?"

"I don't know," Peter answered John. "With lassos, I suppose. Not just single ropes, that's too difficult. But we could have a rope fastened at each side of the entrance, and then two people gallop across with it and then encircle them. It might work."

"But you'd hurt the ponies just as much that way," complained John.

"Yes, I suppose we might. I know, we'll have a rope across at rider's height. Oh no, they'd see it in daytime." Peter thought hard. "We could have two collapsible fences," he said, "and raise them when the enemy's between."

"That's a good idea," said Jane.

"They'd have to be too high to jump, of course," added Jane.

"We'll cover them with grass and stuff, so that they don't recognize them."

"But when can we make them?" asked Pat. "They'll see us unless we get up very early."

Just at that moment Mrs. Hever came in to say that tea was ready.

"And by the way," she added, laughing, "no one's getting up too early to-morrow. It'll probably still be raining, and you'll all have colds, by the look of you."

"How much did you hear of that conversation?" asked Peter, hoping it was not much, and looking at Pat.

"Oh, only the last sentence. More dark plans afoot, I suppose?"

" Yes, but I expect we can tell you." Pat turned to Peter. " Can I, Peter?"

" Well, I suppose so. You won't do anything about it, will you?" he pleaded.

" No, all right," Mrs. Hever laughed.

" Well, we're fighting some enemies, who bashed up our hide—Oh, I forgot!" Pat stopped in horror.

" Oh, go on, tell her," Peter grinned.

" They bashed up our hideout," went on Pat, " the one we've made on the far side of those woods. We've rebuilt it and declared war, and now we want to trap them between two fences."

Peter explained the ambush more carefully, and Mrs. Hever thought for a minute.

" I shouldn't," she said. " You want to capture them when they're on foot. I should capture their ponies first, and then have a hand-to-hand fight. But Jane had better keep guard over their ponies during the fight."

" Oh no!" said Jane quickly.

" No, Jane, you're not to get ill again. Yesterday was quite enough."

" Gosh, Mum, it's a jolly good idea!"

" I'll say!" said John gleefully. He loved a fight.

" One last word," said Mrs. Hever firmly. " Any cavalry with colds will stay indoors to-morrow, and all of you if it's raining like it is to-day."

" Righto," said Jill. She felt tired, but not a bit *coldified*! Then Mrs. Hever chivvied them all in to tea.

After tea Jill managed to tell Peter about riding Prince in the string halter, and about his exemplary behaviour. Then the others came in, and they drew maps to illustrate tactics, and considered all the possible places to find the enemy.

·   ·   ·   ·   ·   ·   ·   ·   ·   ·

After breakfast the next morning it was still raining, but less heavily. No one had a cold, and although Jill had sneezed once or twice, she swore that they were only normal early-morning sneezes. Anyway, they all had to stay in. Peter made a sort of before-battle speech to them thus:

" Now, our plans are as follows: To have a base in the woods behind the enemy's position, and to have a scout on the edge of the wood. We must get there early to-morrow morning or after lunch to-day. Then we watch to see which way they go, and follow. They're bound to stop and camp somewhere, unless they're getting provisions from the village. We leave our horses in Jane's charge, and creep up to capture theirs. Then we four leap on them and tie them up."

That plan was adopted, and Pat added this suggestion to it:

" We must try to find out how many allies they've got, and if they're too many, to capture them without the allies there. They can't always be together."

" Hear, hear," said John noisily.

" The rain's stopped, and the sky's clearing," said Jill, from the window.

" Oh, good," said Peter. " We can start this afternoon. Anyone with a cold?"

" No!" they all shouted, and then leapt out of the door and rushed into the kitchen. Mrs. Hever was there, talking to cook.

" Can we take lunch out?" asked Pat quickly. " No one's got a cold, and it's stopped raining."

" Well, yes, I suppose so. You must all wear macs, though."

Half an hour later, ponies groomed and saddled, lunch and tea packed on their backs, the children started out.

An hour after that, they took up their position behind

the enemy's cottage, and having haltered the ponies farther
back in the wood, they sat down to wait beneath the outer
trees. They talked softly, for fear their voices should carry,
and kept their eyes alert for any sign of the enemy.

After some time they had lunch, and were beginning to

THE ENEMY AT THE FORD

despair, when they saw the eldest enemy, Ann, come out of
the cottage and whistle the ponies. The three sturdy Dart-
moors trotted up to her, for they never wandered far, and
she led them into a shed at one side of the cottage. Five
minutes later all the enemies reappeared, mounted the
ponies, and trotted up the valley. Meanwhile Jane and
Jill had fetched their five ponies, and they all had mounted
and remained in cover. Now they followed the enemy at a
similar pace, keeping just within the woods.

After some time, in which Peter never lost sight of the enemy, they came to some woods which lay on either side of the stream, and which were thick and almost impenetrable. The enemy crossed the stream and plunged boldly into the woods through a very narrow break in the undergrowth.

When our side followed them, at a safe distance, they discovered a well-beaten track that led almost straight through the woods.

" Suppose they look back?" said John.

" We must risk it," said Peter, and cantered after the enemy, still in sight and cantering steadily.

After a few minutes, the enemy suddenly disappeared, and Peter signalled his cavalry to walk. They slowed up.

" They've vanished," he said. " They've either turned into another path or laid a trap. Let's go on again."

They approached the place where they were last seen, and discovered another, narrower path. A few yards along it, it seemed to widen into a clearing, but after that they could see no more. Peter sent John to scout round, and find out if the enemy were still in the clearing.

John came back and reported that the three ponies were tied up to a tree, but that their enemies were not in sight.

" Oh, well," said Peter, shrugging his shoulders, " if they've laid a trap it won't matter. We can use their attack on us to capture them."

" I shouldn't," said Jill. " They may have met allies here. We must find out where they are first. I know," she went on, " let's send a decoy over the other side, and when their attention's distracted, nip in and get the ponies, then rush over to join in the fray."

" Ooh, yes," said John. " I'll go over, make a noise of some sort, and then climb a tree till you arrive."

Peter agreed, and sent Jane to tie up their own horses

ome way down the ride. As Jane returned, they heard
John crashing and shouting over the other side.

"Enough noise for ten," whispered Jane to Jill. Jill
nodded.

"Sh!" said Peter sternly. They waited. Suddenly a
cry rang out through the forest. "Moors forever! Charge!"
And then there was more crashing, and five children came
out of the woods on the opposite side, behind Peter's army.
They were the three known enemies and two others, a boy
and girl of about eleven and twelve.

Peter swung round and began to fight the eldest boy.
Jill and Jane tackled Ann, and Pat went for the new girl.
That left the twins to their own devices, and they began to
run towards the five ponies, to capture them. But John had
heard the fighting, and running towards it, had collected the
enemy's ponies on the way, so the twins rushed at him and
tried to get them back, but John urged them into a canter,
and took them through the wood to the other side. The
twins followed slowly, and John met them as he returned
to the fray on the bay pony.

"I've tied your ponies up on the other side," he shouted,
as he galloped past. They scowled at him, and began to
run to get their ponies back.

When John got back to the battle, he found that Ann
was being successfully tied up, and that Jill and Jane were
just dealing with the strange girl. Peter was, however,
having difficulty with the new boy, and John threw himself off
the bay pony to help.

"Hey!" shouted the new boy, "two against one!"

"All's fair in love and war!" panted Peter, rushing at
his opponent again. Soon all the enemy present had been
dealt with, and safely tied up.

"The twins'll be arriving soon," said John, panting,

and with a light of battle in his eye. " But they'll be on horseback, so we'll need two to one."

" I'll tie up the bay pony with ours," puffed Jane, who felt very tired. She went off down the ride, leading the bay mare, who was sweating.

" Don't you hurt my little Berry," said Ann menacingly, wriggling in her bonds, and looking up the ride for her brothers.

" Here they come," said Peter joyously as hoof-beats thudded on the wet turf, and the twins galloped down the ride, longing for a fight.

They got one all right! As soon as they jumped off on to John and Peter, the two boys shouted: " Leave them to us !" Then a fierce battle raged for several minutes, neither side gaining much. After that, the opponents separated to draw breath, and then engaged in two separate duels. Peter dealt with his man, and then turned to find that the other twin had tied John up, much to the young jockey's disgust.

Then Peter and the remaining twin fought it out, both being too tired to bother much. Peter in the end pinned him to earth, and Pat came to tie him up. After that the two sides made peace and untied all prisoners. They shared all their food and signed peace documents, and then just chatted.

CHAPTER XIV

An Unlucky Discovery

The ten children decided to share the hideout, and led by Pat and Ann, who knew the moor, they all cantered across the moorland towards it. Ann explained that their father was an actor, and had recently bought the cottage, and that she had been sent home from school at half-term because someone had caught measles. She had been able to get to know the moor in that time, and had bought the ponies soon after going there first. Her two allies were some friends who were staying in the village. Their hired ponies had been hidden on the other side of the path.

When they reached the hideout, Peter proudly showed them the racecourse and swimming-pool, and told the ex-enemies about his own army.

After that it was time to go home, and the two parties separated, promising to meet the next afternoon, if it were not wet, at the hideout.

When they got home the whole story was told to Mrs. Hever, who listened with deep interest.

" Oh, good!" she exclaimed. " I knew you'd win, if you tried. Was the bay mare nice to ride, John?"

" Oh yes," he said, with enthusiasm, " ever so fast, and comfortable; and a good mouth, but—but not so good as Bess," he finished up, stoutly loyal.

" Good old John!" said Peter. Everyone laughed.

" Well, it's time you thought about that Horse Show now. It's only three weeks ahead the day after to-morrow."

Mrs. Hever drew two schedules and several entry-forms out of her pocket as she spoke. " Look at those for a bit."

Jill and Jane grabbed one, and Peter the other. John looked over Peter's shoulder, and Pat shared the girls'. Peter read out the classes:

" Best Heavy Hunter—Best Hack—Best Pony under 13 hands; under 15 hands—Best Lightweight Hunter—Best Driving Turnout—Best Child Rider under 12 years; under 17 years—Open Jumping—Child's Jumping under 13 hands and 12 years; then Novice; then under 15 hands and 17 years—Touch and Out. Well, well, five Jumpings. Then Musical Chairs, oh, under 13—Open Bending and Obstacle Race under 17. Pretty good show, sixteen classes."

" Yes, it's super," said Pat.

" Which are you going in for?" Jane asked Jill.

" I don't know much about it," Jill answered.

" Well, let's take down our names and entries," said Peter. " It's nearly time to send them in."

They sat down round the table and decided what to enter for. They were all entering in one or other of the Best Pony, Best Rider and Child's Jumping classes. John was entering in the Musical Chairs, and all five in the Obstacle Race. Mrs. Hever promised Peter and Pat a mount each in the Hack class, and also in the Novice Jumping. Mrs. Hever said that all of them except John and Jane could enter for the Open Bending.

" You'll need a lot of training on Freddy," she warned Jill. " He's very good at it, but pulls terribly."

They completed their entry-forms and stuck them in an envelope with the money. Mrs. Hever had entered all of her horses, except Jigger, for some class or other. The total sum exacted was rather large. Mrs. Hever said laughingly that she hoped they would win it back again.

" Don't worry," said Peter rashly, " we will." He grinned confidently.

Later in the evening he and Jill discussed Prince.

" Couldn't we tell Mrs. Hever now?" asked Jill. " My conscience is pricking."

" No," said Peter persuasively, " let's go on a little longer. Prince must learn to carry other riders. And when he can jump we'll tell her. She'll be more impressed if he shows the same jumping brilliancy as his sire."

" All right," said Jill, but she sighed. It seemed so unnecessary to continue with the secrecy and difficulty.

" Let's get up at 5.30," said Peter, "—if it's light then."

" Oh no !" Jill groaned; " we must have some sleep." But as it happened, Pat developed a cold, and Mrs. Hever said that she must stay in bed until at least 11 o'clock, and so there was only John to be got out of the way. Peter asked Jane to take John a long way away for a ride, and then the coast was clear for them to train Prince until 7.30, because Mr. and Mrs. Hever never got up till then. They arranged to get up at 6 o'clock, and Peter borrowed Jane's alarm clock again.

The next morning was fine, and promised to be hot, and Jill was awake early. She dressed quickly and then, as it was not 6 o'clock, leaned out of her window and revelled in the view and air. She did not feel at all tired, despite the exertions of the day before.

When Peter knocked at her door soon after six, he was feeling very lively too, and had already dressed. They hurried out of the house and down to the stables, and then ran down to the fields. Prince had been turned out again, and was looking very sprightly. Jill saddled him and mounted in a very short space of time, and Peter got up on to Bracken.

" Let's go for a ride by the river," said Peter, longing for a good gallop on Bracken.

" All right," Jill agreed, and they cantered through the open gates down to the river. A path ran along beside this little strip of water, and stretched for some way without any obstacle.

" Let's gallop," suggested Peter, " but keep them together, so that they can't kick or get out of hand." Jill took a firm hold on Prince's snaffle bridle, and they started to canter, gradually increasing speed. Both the animals were fresh, and reached for the bit, tossing their heads, but Peter controlled Bracken's speed, and Jill kept Prince level with Bracken, and they swung along in perfect control.

" Can Prince go out a bit more?" asked Peter rather breathlessly, and increased Bracken's speed. Prince leapt forward and drew level again. Jill found that he was getting out of control and wanted to race.

" Heh! slow down!" she puffed, pulling gently at the bit. Prince drew up easily, and Peter circled Bracken to make him stop.

" That's jolly good," he said to Jill; " he's not even too excited."

Jill found the Arab excited enough. He danced sideways, flicked his heels, and threw his head up frequently.

" He's enjoying the ride," laughed Peter. " I expect he's thinking what fun humans really are. It's good for him to have a change from serious training, anyhow."

Jill nodded, but was too busy hanging on, as Prince half reared, to say anything.

They turned back and started to trot. Prince began to calm down again, and did not buck until they pulled up, and then only once.

Back in the practice field, Jill rode Prince round and

round in a circle, while Peter shouted directions. Prince disliked this restriction, and began to buck. Jill could not calm him, and he bucked harder. She flew off his back and landed on her side. Peter dismounted quickly and ran over to her.

"You all right?" he asked anxiously.

"Yes," said Jill, "I've bruised myself a bit." She jumped up and grinned at Peter. "Not so badly as when I slid down that slope!" Peter laughed, and mounted Bracken. Jill went over and caught Prince, who was standing quietly, obviously regretting his wild behaviour.

Jill mounted him again, and walked him round in the same circle. He submitted, but looked sulky, and Peter soon suggested that they should leave him alone and go back to the house.

.   .   .   .

Unfortunately, just after they had returned from their ride by the river, Pat had woken up, and having a very heavy cold, had gone down to the kitchen to make a lemon drink. She was not supposed to get out of bed, really, but she hated staying in bed all day, and wanted to move about while she could, before her mother was up. All the bedrooms faced south or east, and as the fields were on the west side of the house, Peter had thought they were safe from discovery although in sight of the house.

The kitchen, however, was on the west side, and therefore, just as she put the kettle on to boil, Pat saw Jill being bucked off. For a moment she was going to run out and stop the training, then she hesitated, and decided not to. She felt annoyed that Jill should attempt to ride the horse that was to be her own when he was trained, and her anger grew exceedingly when she saw Jill remount and ride him round successfully.

JILL'S TURN FOR A TOSS

" I must think how to stop their plans," she thought.
" I had suspected it, but it seemed impossible. If they succeed with him, as they almost have, Mum will probably
let Jill have Prince, and I want him so much. He's a really
super horse, and we'd win lots of prizes. But I must plot
carefully, so that they get into trouble about it, then I can
have him."

.   .   .   .

Pat could think of no scheme, and life went on appar-
ently smoothly for a few days. The children met their erst-
while enemies several times, and got on well with them.
In the mornings they practised hard under the eye of Mrs.
Hever, and their riding improved steadily in this way.
They no longer rode about rather slackly, but always
remembered to sit up well, and did not let the ponies move
uncollectedly.

Jill and Peter found little time for Prince, and could do
no more than keep him from forgetting what he already
knew. Jill loved the pony more and more and, like Pat,
could not bear the thought that he might belong to someone
else.

The weather was very hot, and each morning dawned
without a cloud in the sky. Soon the stream began to dry
up, and then the grass wilted, and Mr. Hever looked up at
the sky anxiously, muttering: " Storm's coming, I'm sure.
Ought to keep the horses in."

He put off bringing them in, however, because under
cover they would need much more care, and he was busy
with his sheep at this time of year, getting them in ready
to fatten for autumn markets.

Pat was still trying to think of a way to stop Jill training
Prince. She was unwilling to tell tales, or to get Jill and
Peter into trouble deliberately, but could think of no way

of stopping them otherwise. She delayed and hesitated, wanting to act, but not knowing what action to take.

During this time Jill had learned to bend on Freddy, and could beat any of the other children in this race.

Pat had decided to ride Freddy in Novice Jumping, for although he was only a pony, he could jump like a stag, and was quite capable of clearing the jumps in that class if he tried. Mrs. Hever gave Peter Firefly to ride in this class, and the boy had to put in much practice on the mare, as she was inexperienced and hot-tempered.

Jill also practised jumping on Freddy, whom she was riding in Child's Jumping. Pat had given Sunny a lot of schooling, and he was now a much better pony. He could jump quite well, although he was not very smooth, and he was quick at gymkhana contests and in turning.

In the evenings during this time Jane had completed two more pictures—of Freddy and of Bracken. Her three pictures now hung on the walls of the barn and looked very well. She had caught the likenesses well; each portrait had a typical expression of its subject.

Mr. Hever thought a lot of the pictures, although he said little, and he asked Jane to paint all the horses as well, when she had finished the five ponies, and everyone knew that such a request meant a real admiration for her skill, and Jane became almost too happy, and hardly dared hope that such a beginning might lead to a great climax. Peter felt very glad for her, and extremely proud.

Several days passed before Pat could think up a plan to stop Jill training Prince; in the end she decided to steal Prince, hide him somewhere in the woods, and then to continue his training herself. Jill could say nothing about his disappearance, for she would feel too guilty herself, and the grown-ups would just think that Prince had run away again. When she could ride him with ease, she would come forward with him, and say that she had trained him. She would explain to Jill that she had been afraid that her mother would be too annoyed at Jill's training him, and so had finished it herself, although she was very grateful for Jill's early work with the colt.

Pat almost went to explain this to Jill at the time, but then remembered how sensible Peter was, and how he would probably say that her mother would not mind at all, and that he was not going to let her walk off with the honour due to him and Jill.

So one night she crept out of the house at about midnight, into the heavy, sullen air, and took a halter from the harness room. Then she ran down to Prince's field, casting anxious glances at the sky, which was troubled and cloudy, and lit up dimly by a red light diffused from the south. She called Prince softly as she shut the gate.

CHAPTER XV

Prince in Trouble

It did not take long to catch Prince, for since Jill's gentle ministrations he had grown much more trustful. Pat led him out of the field, and then shut the gate carefully. Prince tossed his head, so she held the rope tighter. Prince disliked this and snapped at her arm. She gave him a tap with the end of his halter rope, as was Mrs. Hever's method with the ponies. Prince, however, was not used to such treatment, and was so surprised that he became very quiet and walked along soberly.

The air grew heavier, the clouds seemed to be getting lower, and Pat felt anxious. She could not leave Prince in the woods during a storm, for he might injure himself in his fear. Pat remembered several occasions when Prince had been badly scared by thunder, and had had to be soothed and comforted even in the stables.

Pat decided to keep him out in the open valley, near the shelter of a hedge if possible. She found a suitably sheltered place, and stopped there just as the first sounds of thunder could be heard in the distance. Prince started nervously, and trembled. Pat stroked his neck and rubbed his ears. He calmed down a little, but as the storm came nearer and the thunder grew louder, he became more and more restive, and refused to let Pat touch his head. She held on to the rope as he half reared, but then the lightning flashed

PAT IN TROUBLE

out, and so did Prince's heels, and in a moment he had pulled free and raced off down the valley.

Pat was absolutely horrified, and for a moment was paralysed with fear, but then Prince suddenly stopped and crouched with his ears laid back. Pat ran towards him, calling him desperately. She saw his eyes shining as the lightning flashed, and then he turned sharply towards the woods, and Pat saw him disappear into the shadows, still rearing and bucking as he went.

She stopped still, and the awful realization of what she had done rushed in on her. He was lost, and lost in the night, in a storm when he might hurt himself, and worst of all, he still had the loose halter rope dangling! Pat ran in the direction he had gone, blindly and wildly, and then she knew suddenly that she would not find him, and fell beneath a tree, sobbing bitterly.

. . . .

Meanwhile Prince was racing along, without direction or purpose, just driven by fear. Each roll of thunder urged him on, and at every flash of lightning he tossed his head wildly and kicked out. Luckily he avoided treading on the halter rope, but he came very near tripping over it in this way, and it was pure luck that he did not break a leg.

Soon he came across a hedge, and in his terror leapt it. He landed badly, and rolled over on to his side, but did not hurt himself, and was soon on his feet again. He stood still for a minute, but then the lightning came again, and he began to race round the field, trampling the corn which was just ready to be harvested. Now he began to whinny and scream with terror, for the field was strange, and he dared not jump out again.

The field was actually quite near Appleby's farm, and the storm, together with the noises Prince was making, brought the old farmer wide awake and out of bed in a very short time. He looked out of the window, and could have screamed too, to see his best field of corn being ruined in this way, just before it was to have been harvested too. He cursed, and reached for his gun. Just as he raised it to his shoulder, however, reason appealed to his enraged senses, and he lowered it.

He remembered that if he killed the animal, he would get no compensation for his destroyed corn, and so he hurriedly threw on some clothes and rushed out of the house. He could not catch Prince, however, until the storm had died away, and the tired colt had calmed down.

Then the angry farmer went and led Prince out. He was not unkind to the animal, because it would do no good, and besides, he could see what terror he had felt, and he pitied the beautiful Arab. He recognized the colt at once, and having shut him up in the stables with some hay and water, he went in and wrote a stiff letter to the Hevers, demanding compensation, and condemning their negligence. Then he went back to bed, and finished his night's sleep.

. . . .

The next morning at the Hevers', everything was quite calm. Pat had come home soon after she had lost Prince, and had lain sleepless on her bed until about six o'clock. Then she got up, and went for a ride on Sunny. She could not see Prince anywhere, and returned in time to help Jill get breakfast.

" I say," she said suddenly as she came into the kitchen, " it's funny, Prince must have got out again."

" Oh, has he!" exclaimed Jill. " I suppose the lightning frightened him. Don't worry, he'll probably come back." Jill's confidence cheered Pat slightly, and she decided to say nothing of her part in the happenings of the night. During breakfast everyone discussed Prince's passion for freedom, and Mrs. Hever said that it was time he was broken in and trained.

During the morning the children rode about in the neighbourhood, and kept their eyes open for Prince. They did not see him, of course, for he was still shut up in Appleby's stables.

In the afternoon they went up to the hideout to meet their friends. The two other children, who had been staying in the village, had gone away the day before, so there were only eight of them.

They first of all told Ann, Bill and Jack about Prince, and they in answer promised to keep a look-out for him. After that Peter explained his racecourse to them, and everyone helped to mark it out with white pegs. Then they made several brush jumps, about 2 ft. 6 in. and 3 ft. high, and nearly 10 ft. wide. Then Peter gave careful orders as to where they should be set up, and in about half an hour he had produced, with seven helpers, of course, a very good model of a real hurdle course.

Peter at once wanted to try Bracken, so he went and mounted the pony, and cantered him round the course, clearing the obstacles easily.

" Now, look," he said as he pulled up again, " we mustn't actually race until the ponies are well schooled, or there'll be trouble. Each of you had better try it alone, and slowly, at first."

So everyone had a try, and declared the course to be very comfortably spaced. The three newcomers rode very well, and their ponies jumped neatly with enthusiasm.

Afterwards they had tea, and then Ann agreed to join their Arab tribe. Pat, still worried about Prince, conceded her rank of second in command to Ann. It seemed a necessary piece of diplomacy, because the three Moors were a lively addition to the tribe, and could fight well.

Then Peter suggested that they should come back to see their headquarters in the barn. On the way, Jill told them

about Jane's beautiful portraits, and tried to forget about
Prince being lost.

When they came to the house after some time, the three
strangers were first of all introduced to Mrs. Hever, and then
hurried over to the barn, where they had left the ponies.
Ann and the twins were suitably impressed by the three
pictures, and looked round in wonder at the walls, hung with
gay mats, and the whole barn, with its homely-looking furniture at one end, and its scanty stables at the other.

It was not a look of scorn, however, and they felt excited
at having found such original friends. Everyone sat down
then, as many as possible on the available seating and the
others on the steps leading to the loft.

" Now," said Peter, when everyone was settled, " let's
discuss things a bit. I'd like to suggest a series of tests, which
give you a certain rank in the tribe. Whoever gets highest
in the series, is chief."

" That's a good idea," said Ann eagerly, " but I can't
think of many tests."

" No, it's rather difficult," agreed Pat. Prince had still
not returned, but she felt less worried now. He would come
back soon.

" Well," suggested Jane, " you could have time tests on
different ponies. You know, a flat race on Bracken, a round
of jumps on Freddy—at least, that would have to be on faults.
And you could have swimming tests too."

" Yes, but where?" asked John. " Not in our pool!"

" That's a good idea, Jane," said Ann. " It's a pity we
can't swim somewhere."

" Look," said Peter, " we ought to have a certain test
on each pony. Of course, we couldn't do anything too
strenuous on Bess, although she is quite strong. I'll write
them down as you all suggest the tests."

" Berry is very good at racing over jumps," said Ann.

" Biscuits has a soft back. You could jump bareback on him," Jack spoke up.

" How about an Obstacle Race?" asked Bill. " Sandy is very quick."

" Bracken'll flat race, then," added Peter. " Silver can Stick the Pig, Jane."

" Righto. What else can we have?" Jane looked round.

" Sunny can do Bending and Potato Race," said Pat.

" Is Freddy going to do a round of jumps?" asked Jill, looking at Pat, who nodded.

" What can Bess do, then?" asked John. " Oh, I know. We can shoot arrows and throw lassos while she gallops. She'll be quiet enough for that."

" Well," said Peter, " let's do some of the tests to-morrow, up at the hideout. We'll meet you there at 2.30. Come and see our other horses now."

Everyone followed him down to the fields.

.   .   .   .

The next morning Jill woke up with a heavy weight on her mind, and yet an urgent feeling of something that had to be done. When she was a little wider awake, she remembered what was bothering her. Prince had still not returned when they had gone to bed the night before, and she must go down now to see if he had returned in the night.

The rain was splattering against the windows again, and outside it was sweeping in sheets over the brilliant green moors. The trees in the woods were swaying, their branches cracking against each other, and Jill could not look out any longer for the thought that Prince might be out there, perhaps injured, with his beautiful coat matted and streaky in the rain, his white fetlocks brown with mud, and his eyes shut against the wind.

She hurried over dressing, and scraped her hair into plaits with all speed. Then she went downstairs quietly and quickly, and put on her mac.

"Oh," she thought, "how lovely if he's there, and comes up to me, and I can pat his neck. He must have returned by now. Oh, Prince, you must have come back!" She went into the kitchen to get some carrots for the wanderer, and then slipped out of the back door. She could not bear to look towards the fields, in case she should see them empty.

When she got to the gate of Prince's usual field, she found Peter there, hunched up with his elbows on the gate.

"Oh, gosh!" she said, fearing the worst, which she guessed from Peter's unhappy-looking position.

Peter swung round. "Oh, it's you, Jill. No, he hasn't come back." Their eyes met, and each read in the other's the awful fear and misery which they felt. The carrots slipped from Jill's hand, and lay forgotten in the mud.

"He might be in the other fields," said Jill, but without hope. Peter nodded, and they plodded round the fields together, finding no black Arab, friendly and running up to them, ready for his usual tit-bit.

They returned to the house, and as it was already 7.30, made themselves a pot of tea, and then decided to give the others some as well. Mrs. Hever always made some in her room, but did not usually give the children any. Jill knew that she would not mind, however, and felt that they needed something warming after the disappointment.

They took up the others' tea, and told them the bad news. Then they went down to the kitchen again, and discussed whether they were to blame for Prince's disappearance.

"I don't really think so," said Peter in the end. "I mean to say, we haven't taught him to jump yet. And we

10   (G 391)

didn't worry him or excite him too much, either. I wonder what's happened."

" So do I," sighed Jill. Then the cook came in, and they helped her get breakfast, by laying the table and watching the toast. She was sympathetic about Prince, but had not known him well, and did not appreciate the loss.

At breakfast, however, something happened to lighten the suspense. Mr. Hever received a hand-delivered letter. He opened it, looked at it for a minute, then read it aloud.

" Dear Sir,

In the storm last night your Arab colt broke loose, and did much damage to my best crop of wheat. You know what that will mean to me, and I would like to discuss compensation, if you will come round on Thursday at 11.0. I intend to hold the animal in custody until you can provide some suitable means for keeping him under control. I shall look after him, and send in a bill.

Yours sincerely,

George Appleby."

" Gosh!" sighed Pat. " Thank heavens he's all right!" And everyone agreed with her.

CHAPTER XVI

Prince Returns

For a few minutes everyone chatted happily, their minds considerably lightened by the good news. Then, however, Mr. Hever spoke again.

"It's pretty serious, though. Heaven knows what he'll want for compensation. I can't refuse him, either."

"And what he said about Prince." Mrs. Hever considered the letter, which her husband had thrown over to her, and then added: "Of course, I suppose we shall have to sell Prince actually. We can't afford to keep him in stables, and anyway, it would be bad for him."

"Oh, Mummy, you can't sell him!" Pat was feeling very relieved, and her spirits were rising rapidly. "Couldn't we make the fences higher in one of the fields? Besides, I expect the storm frightened him."

"Yes, perhaps you're right, but he got out before, in the fog. I'm afraid he's got rather a wanderlust at the moment." Mrs. Hever felt that he was a bit too much to cope with.

"Oh, gosh," said Peter, "but he's a super horse! He'll be marvellous when he's trained." Peter saw all his plans for his first success in training going wrong, and knew how Jill must be feeling.

"Well, we'll have to see," said Mr. Hever thoughtfully. "I can't really pay out £50 each time Prince feels like going for a stroll."

"Will it be as much as that?"

" Might be more. Depends how much damage he did. It's a shame for Appleby, he'd banked a lot on that corn. It's his most valuable crop, really."

.   .   .   .

That afternoon the rain had stopped, although the sky was overcast and the air damp, and so Peter set out with his cavalry for the hideout, to meet their new members. They did not take tea, for Mrs. Hever had said that it was too wet to stay out long, and that they must ask the others back to tea. When they cantered into the clearing, the others were already there. They had brought tea with them, but willingly accepted the Hevers' invitation and at once shared what they had brought. John for one was never tired of eating, and the others ran him close.

When Pat told Ann about Prince's escape, and Appleby's holding of him, Ann was horrified that they had not yet taken strong measures to get the animal back.

" I should go and raid his stables," she averred stoutly. " I mean to say, he's your horse."

" Yes, but he doesn't want any more damage done. It's quite reasonable."

" One can see his point of view, but I vote we try to get Prince back. It'd be fun, anyway. Something to keep your army in trim, Peter."

" Oh yes. But we mustn't hurt the animal, getting him away. Well, I suppose we could." Peter thought for a moment. " How could we?"

" Well, we could break in when Appleby's not there, or trick him into giving us the key, or something."

" I know," said Jane; " let's go and spy round his farm now, and if we can, just lead Prince back home."

" All right," cried Peter. " To horse!"

They leapt on to their ponies, and galloped up the valley

and through the wood. When they were nearer the farm, they slowed up and went cautiously. They left the ponies tied to the fence of the field next to Appleby's stable-yard. Then Peter led the way, and walked boldly round the yard.

There was no sign of the farmer, and the party grew confident. All the doors round the yard were shut—Peter tried them one by one.

"No good on that side," he murmured, "probably grain-sheds." The next door opened, however, and Peter saw bulky shapes moving uneasily in the half-light, worried by the strange smell of a human being they did not know. One of them mooed softly, and Peter withdrew again.

"No good," he said, "cows——"

"What are you doing!" roared the farmer, coming out of the shed suddenly. "What do you want? Oh, it's you. If you're wanting the horse, you can't have him back until he's properly guarded. My best field of grain," he muttered as he finished.

"Can we just see him, please?" asked Pat as sweetly as she could.

"I don't trust you," Appleby answered. "Likely as not, you'd rush in and take him away again. No, you'd all better go home and keep out of mischief."

"Come on, we'd better go," said Peter to Ann, who was looking rebellious. They all walked out and mounted their ponies again, watched by the enraged farmer. They felt annoyed too.

. . . .

At tea that day Pat told her mother that the farmer would not even let them see Prince.

"That's mean," she said, but laughed and added: "He probably couldn't trust you! By the way, we've decided to keep Prince in stables for a bit until we settle what to do, and he may just as well be at home as in Appleby's stables. Daddy'll tell him so to-morrow when he goes over to discuss terms."

" Oh, good !" exclaimed Pat. All the children were pleased, even Ann and her brothers, who had never seen Prince.

" By the way, Jill," said Mrs. Hever suddenly, " your parents are coming the day after to-morrow. We'll all go and meet the train you came on, I think. My arm's much less stiff now. I should be able to drive."

" How did you do it?" asked Ann sympathetically.

" Oh, trying to train the notorious Prince," she laughed. The five who knew him smiled.

" Is he very hot?" asked Bill.

" Yes, he is rather. His skin's very sensitive, and he hates any pressure on his back." Jill looked at Peter. They grinned. Suddenly Jill realized that Pat had intercepted the look and was grinning too, in a nice way.

As soon as they had an opportunity, after their three friends had gone, Jill and Peter found Pat to talk to her, while Jane began her portrait of Bess, with John looking on.

" It's all right," said Pat, laughing. " I know what you've been doing, and I want to help if I can." She became more serious, and went on: " As a matter of fact, I've a confession to make. When I saw you training him one morning, I felt mad, because he was supposed to have been going to be my horse, only we couldn't train him."

" Oh gosh, Pat," said Jill quickly, " I'm awfully sorry !"

" Oh no, Jill, it's all right. If you were able to, there's no reason why you shouldn't have trained him. Anyway, I planned to hide him in the wood and finish his training myself."

JANE PAINTS A PORTRAIT

Light dawned on the other two.

" Yes," went on Pat, " you've guessed. I took him out in the night of the storm, and he was frightened, and escaped."

" Gosh, you must have felt awful when he didn't come back!" said Jill.

" I did! But anyway, now I'm ready to help you get him trained, and if we can stop Mum selling him, I'll get her to let you have him."

" Good old Pat!" said Peter, slapping her on the back.

" Do you mean really my own?" asked Jill, almost inarticulate with joy.

"Of course, silly," said Pat, swallowing hastily with sorrow at giving the colt away, and going on: "I'm not really fit to have him, and you understand him much better. Anyway, we shall both lose him if we don't think of something. We'd better tell Mum that I led him out that night, and that you have been getting on well with him, and maybe she'll keep him."

"Oh no, Pat," said Peter firmly, "we're not getting you into trouble over this. She'd be awfully mad with you."

"I know, but what else can we do?" Pat's mind could not think of anything, it was ready to accept defeat.

"Well," said Jill, "we must just think of something. It'll come soon."

.   .   .   .

The next day Mr. Hever went over to Appleby. They discussed the damage, went and inspected the field in question, and finally agreed on a sum for compensation. Mr. Hever said how sorry he was about it, and Appleby replied that he was glad they had settled it so amicably.

"Well," said Mr. Hever carefully, "there's just one thing still. Look, I agree to keep the animal in stables as long as he's with me. We're thinking of selling him, you know. Of course, if he does settle down we shall want to keep him. He's a jolly good horse, really."

"Yes!" agreed the farmer. "He's always good-tempered when I go in to feed him, but he kicks and bites if I try to clean out his box, or brush the mud off his coat."

"Does he? He's always been quiet before. Well, shall I fetch him this afternoon?"

"Yes, if you like, Mr. Hever."

"I'll come round about three, then. See you later, Mr. Appleby."

"Righto, Mr. Hever. Good-day to you!"

Mr. Hever walked out into the yard and mounted Nagina, whom he had ridden over. He felt annoyed that Appleby had been exciting Prince, although he said nothing. Nagina had smelt her son through the doors of the stables, and was unwilling to leave the place, but Mr. Hever firmly headed her for home, and set her cantering over the field.

At lunch he told the family what had happened. The children were delighted, and Jill longed to see the colt again. She could hardly eat, and as soon as lunch was over, she went to the stables and began to tidy up one of the boxes for Prince. It happened to be one just visible from her room, and it was well placed for light and air. She swept it carefully, laid down generous heaps of sawdust, and then smoothed them to make a level surface.

" Hullo !" said a voice from the doorway. It was John, who had just been told how Jill had won Prince's confidence, and was brimming over with admiration, and wanted to know how she had done it.

So while she cleaned the cobwebs and dust off the windows, brought in a bucket of water and some hay, she told John all that had happened. Soon the other three came along to see Prince's new box, and to discuss how to get Mrs. Hever to keep him.

" I say," said Peter with surprise, " you've got the box Nag has in bad weather, when he's in. It doesn't matter, but it just struck me that you've picked the best one!" Everyone laughed, and Jill looked rather sheepish.

" Anyway," said Peter seriously, " we must think hard for a plan now." They leant against the walls, and for some time discussed the problem. They could think of no solution.

" Even if we do get him perfectly trained," said Jane thoughtfully, " they won't know for sure that he won't break out again. What we want to do, is to show them in some test of training."

" Gosh, Jane, that's it!" Jill stepped forward. " Look, we can enter him for something in the Show."

This bombshell produced a stunned silence.

" But, Jill," said Peter reasonably, " how can we enter him without letting Mrs. Hever know? Oh, I see! Enter him on the day. No, it's impossible. The only event you can enter for at the last minute is one of the Jumpings."

" It *is* an idea," said Pat. " Think how pleased Mum would be! But then suppose he made a scene in the ring? That would make matters worse! Besides, he can't jump yet."

Jill's face was pale and set with determination as she said forcefully: " Look, all of you, it's our only chance of keeping Prince. Think what might happen to him if he were sold to the wrong people! And I say we've just got to teach him to jump. After all, he jumps beautifully already, it's only a matter of—of—co-ordinating his abilities."

" Yes, I see what you mean," Peter agreed thoughtfully. " But he's not used to crowds or show jumps."

" Well, then, he's got to learn!" Pat caught on to Jill's idea with enthusiasm. " Jill, how can we get him to the Show unseen, and hide him when he's there?"

" Oh, gosh!" groaned Jill, her hopes crumbling a little, sickeningly.

" It's all right!" exclaimed Peter joyfully. " Tim'll help us! You know, the ex-jockey we met at the races. I know where he is, and I'll write to him. He'll take Prince in his lot of horses!"

. . . .

The next day Jill drove off with her host and hostess to meet her parents. Mr. Hever had put his foot down about Mrs. Hever driving with her arm still in plaster. There was room for only one child, who naturally had to be Jill.

The drive was a pleasant one, as the weather was mild and sunny, and Dartmoor looked at its best. They arrived in plenty of time to meet the train, and wandered about the station trying the penny-in-the-slot machines. At last the train steamed in, and Jill remembered the day, about a month ago, that she had felt so excited when she had arrived.

Mr. and Mrs. Crewe jumped out of their compartment, and stretched after their long journey. Then they saw Jill, and hurried over to meet her and the Hevers.

" How are you, Ann? Has Jill been too bad? It's kind of you——"

" Well, Jill, you have grown, I think. And you look very fit. How's she behaved herself, Bill?"

And so it went on. Jill kissed her parents, and at last managed to get the four chattering grown-ups out to the car. Soon they had got the luggage in, and were speeding along the roads back to the house.

Mrs. Crewe told her daughter that her father had now got a job in Plymouth, and wanted to buy a house somewhere near. She was surprised how healthy and happy Jill looked, and wondered whether they should always live on Dartmoor. Mr. Crewe said it would be a good idea, and that they could keep horses. Jill was, of course, thrilled by all this.

CHAPTER XVII

Training is Continued

Meanwhile Peter and the others had written a letter to Tim, explaining what had happened, and begging him to help them.

"Suppose he gives us away?" asked Pat.

"I don't think he will," explained Peter. "He's a jolly decent sort, and likes us."

After a day there, Jill's parents were thoroughly taken with the idea of living on Dartmoor, and got into touch with an estate agent, to try to find a suitable house near the Hevers. They decided to let their place in London.

There was now only a bare two weeks before the Show, and Jill was snatching all opportunities to train Prince. Nearly every day Mr. Hever was out on the moor finding and selecting sheep for the autumn fair. And nearly every day Jill's parents were looking at houses in the neighbourhood, usually accompanied by Mrs. Hever. All the children were in the secret, so whenever all the grown-ups were out except for cook, who did not count, they dashed down to the stables, and all saddled their ponies while Jill got Prince ready.

At first he had to relearn his previous training, for the storm and strange stalls had made him restless and nervy. Peter encouraged the others to ride about during his training, so that he should be used to the crowds and other animals when the day came.

After a couple of days' training, Peter said that he was

ready to start jumping, and they planned to begin his serious preparation the next morning, before the grown-ups awoke.

Jill went to sleep very excited, and dreamt strange things which she could not remember when she woke up. It was early in the morning, and the room was only half-light. Wide awake at once, she jumped out of bed, went to the window and called Prince. He put his head out over the half-door of his box and nickered.

Jill dressed quickly and plaited her hair. Then she went along and knocked softly at Peter's door. He groaned and said that he would not be long, so Jill tiptoed down the stairs and out of the back door, and ran over to the stables. She collected Prince's saddle and bridle from the harness room, and went to his box to saddle him. He greeted her with a friendly push of his nose, and moved back as she shut the door behind her. She gave his coat a perfunctory brush, and smoothed his soft mane down on the right side of his neck. Then she threw the reins over his neck and slipped the bit into his mouth; next she did up the throat-lash. She was just lifting the saddle to put it on his back when Peter appeared in the doorway.

" I'll go and get some low jumps ready," he whispered; " you follow as soon as you're finished. Only don't mount him till you get to the field." Peter disappeared again.

Two minutes later Jill led Prince across the yard. Luck-ily it was rather muddy, and the noise of hooves was muffled. When they got inside the field, Jill pulled the girths up a little tighter and mounted. While Peter finished fixing the bar as low as possible in the posts, Jill cantered Prince round the field once, and then stood still to get orders from Peter.

" Canter him up to it slowly from that brush jump, and

then give him his head. But I should keep a hand on his mane in case he jumps awkwardly or refuses." The boy stood back at the side of the jump.

Jill walked Prince over to the side of the brush jump, and started him cantering. She held him straight and at a slow canter. He pricked his ears at the jump, and seemed quite at home with the idea. Three yards from the jump Jill threw her hands forward, and let her body follow, still sitting down in the saddle. Her head was to one side of the colt's neck as he rose to clear the jump. The excited girl hardly noticed the landing, and as soon as Prince had been pulled in to a standstill, she turned him round and made him do it again.

Several times the black colt jumped it, eagerly and with plenty to spare, until Peter was satisfied.

" I'll put it up to 1 ft.," he called. Jill sat still on Prince while he did so, and talked softly to the colt, who was mouthing the bit and impatient for more. He hardly felt Jill's weight.

The Arab found 1 ft. no difficult obstacle, and cleared it several times.

" What's he like?" asked Peter as he put the jump up to 1 ft. 6 in.

" Very comfortable," Jill answered. " It's absolutely effortless."

Prince had to spring a little more to clear the higher jump, and he began to feel the weight of a rider. After the first jump over 1 ft. 6 in. he began to sweat, and Jill rested him for a minute. When she tried him again, he refused, and Jill made him look at it well before jumping from a standstill, which he did unwillingly, and knocking the bar with a hind leg.

" Just make him jump it once more, properly, and we'd

PRINCE REFUSES

better stop," said Peter. So Jill set him at the jump. When
he almost refused again, Jill kicked him lightly, and in
his surprise the colt leapt over nimbly. After that Jill dismounted and hooked the reins over a post. She and Peter
watched the pony and discussed his training.

"We must have a plan," said Peter seriously. "We
have ten days left, counting to-day. Now, this afternoon
he can try two or three small jumps one after the other.
To-morrow he must jump higher, and the day after higher
still. Then the jumps must be more complicated. On the
tenth day, which is just before the Show, you know, he
must have a contest with Bracken and Freddy. He should
be all right by then; it's only experience he wants now."

"Let's try a round of small jumps now," said Jill; "we
must get on to the bigger jumps quickly, or he won't have
enough practice at them."

"All right, then," Peter agreed, and they put up three
1 ft. jumps about ten yards apart, and then Prince had to
jump them all several times before he had a last reminder
of his aids, and was returned to the stable, where he drank
deeply. Jill wiped his neck and legs dry, and then helped
Peter clean the tack, so that no one should see it had been
used.

Before breakfast they told the others how well he had
got on, and Jill was in a daze all the early part of the morning until the grown-ups had all left to see some houses,
and they could train Prince again.

This time he jumped 2 ft., and tackled four jumps in
succession. Jill began to feel how well he responded to the
new task, and the other children were surprised to see how
readily he obeyed Jill. The same afternoon he had still
another lesson, and tried a 2 ft. 6 in. jump, which he easily
cleared.

" You mustn't strain him by doing too much," warned the careful Pat.

" Well," Peter explained, " we're only giving him short lessons with some time between each. I think he'll take it all right, but you'd better inspect him before each exercise, to make sure he's fit. You are the vet. in our tribe, you know."

" How high are the Novice jumps?" asked John.

" Not higher than 4 ft.," said Pat. " Probably not that much."

" Gosh," said Jill, looking at the 4 ft. peg on the post beside her. " It looks high enough to me."

" Yes," laughed Peter, " but Prince'll jump that easily soon. To-morrow he can try a white jump!"

. . . .

The next day, as Peter promised, Prince was introduced to a plain, white-painted bar. He was very suspicious, and Jill let him look all round it well before making him jump. At first he refused about five yards away from the jump, and then decided, with a little persuasion from Jill's heels, to get it over with, and he jumped it perfectly.

It had been at 1 ft. and Peter said that she must get him used to the new kind of jump before raising it. Several times Prince refused, but each time Jill dealt with him patiently and sympathetically, but made him go over, and in the end he was jumping it fearlessly.

Then Jill made him jump the brush at 1 ft. 6 in. He enjoyed the natural kind of jump and went over it well up to 2 ft. 6 in. Then he was taken back to the stables. Later on in the day he came out for two more exercises, and at the end was jumping 3 ft. 6 in. over the plain bar, the brush and the white bar.

" I say," said Peter, as Jill walked Prince round to cool

off, " he does get rather tired. Do you think we could feed him a few oats, Pat?"

" Well, yes, I expect so. He would more easily stand up to this training then. He gets much too tired now. But we can't give him many unless we buy them ourselves. Oh, but of course, it's only for a few days. Dad wouldn't notice that, and afterwards he won't mind. We could give him one pound a day."

" Oh, good!" said Peter. " Well, Jill, things are moving, and we certainly will have a chance to win it, I believe."

That evening, after her father had shut the horses up for the night, Pat went out and gave Prince his supper of oats. The young horse had not had many before, and was delighted. They had decided that this was the only time to give it him, as otherwise Mr. Hever would be about or the time would be too near an exercise.

" To-morrow morning," murmured Peter to Jill as they cleared the supper dishes to help Cook, " he'll be very fresh after those oats, and I want you to try him straight-away on a reasonable round of jumps. We'll have a 3 ft. bar, a 2 ft. 6 in. brush, and a 2 ft. white bar. That should wake him up!"

Jill went to bed with trepidation in her heart. She felt that Prince would stand or fall by his performance the next day.

.   .   .   .

The next day dawned fine and clear, and Jill was up early, getting Prince ready. Peter had got down before her, and was setting up the little round of jumps. He had saddled Bracken too, and when Jill got down to the field, he was practising the jumps and cantering round the field on Bracken, who was very fresh and kept pulling for his head.

" Gosh," Jill called, " the jumps look awfully high!   I hope he can do them."   She put her foot in the stirrup and swung into Prince's saddle.

" Oh, they aren't too bad," said Peter, cantering up. Jill pulled her girth up another hole and grinned.

" He does stand well now," said Peter admiringly, " and he's quiet when you tighten the girths too.   I think he's getting very good manners."

" Hm," agreed Jill.   She made Prince canter round the field, and then set him at the first jump, the plain bar. The colt pricked his ears and sailed over easily.   The next jump was a white bar, quite low, and Prince found no difficulty in clearing that.   He still disliked the colour of the jump, but did not fear it.   Then Jill had to circle him, which she did slowly, and then steady him to take the brush.

He disliked the turn between the two jumps, and did not face the jump straight as he cantered at it.   The result was that he rose badly, and made an awkward jump with a bad landing.   It was all Jill could do to stay on, and Peter made them practise cantering in a circle after that, with two low jumps, one on each side of the circle, so that they had to turn half a circle between each.

Later in the day Prince tried the 4 ft. jump, and cleared it quite easily.   Jill's riding was also improving with this training, and she looked very much a part of her horse as they jumped, she lying over the colt's neck as he rose.

They also tried another round with nothing higher than 3 ft., and Prince got used to any combination of the three types of jumps that he knew.   By the end of the day he was jumping all of them singly at 4 ft. and all three together at 3 ft.

Peter was very pleased, and all the children extremely excited.

That afternoon Peter got a letter from Tim. He called the others and they assembled in the barn.

" Listen," he said, and began to read it out:

" Dear Peter,

Thank you for your letter. I was interested to hear about Prince. I think I shall be able to take him with my lot. There are only three horses going from our stables, and we're using two horse-boxes. There should be room in one of them for Prince. Luckily the owner is going ahead by car, so it should not be difficult to leave your animal hidden in the horse-box during the whole Show, while the other three are outside. He won't enjoy it much, I am afraid, but we must hide him. One thing, though, I want to make sure I'm not helping you in some silly enterprise, and I want to come over some time before the Show to see him jump a real show-round. I hope you're getting him used to people and other horses. Would 7th Sept. be all right? That's two days before the Show. He should be ready by then, you know!

Yours, Tim Brierly."

" Gosh," said Jane, " it's the 1st to-day!"

" Is it really?" exclaimed Pat and Peter together. " We've got to move fast," Peter added.

" I hope he'll learn quickly," sighed Jill. " I suppose we've got five complete days before Tim comes. But he's got to learn wall, in and out, and triple bar yet."

CHAPTER XVIII

Days of Anxiety

While they were busy training Prince, of course, the children were also carrying on their lawful practice for the Show. Jill was practising Jumping and Bending on Freddy, and all the rest were working hard on their own ponies. Pat had also to practise on Freddy for the Novice, and Jill thrilled to think of herself and Pat competing together in that class. Peter was riding in it too, of course, on Firefly, and all three foresaw a good competition.

" I wonder what else is entered for Novice," Peter often said. " Of course there'll be a lot of long-legged raw thoroughbred stuff, which isn't much danger. Then there'll be some useful animals who've been well trained, and are just preparing to enter for the Open classes. I must say, it's lucky your father isn't entering himself, or he'd see Prince and stop him competing." He turned to Pat in the last part of this speech, and she agreed.

They saw their friends only once before the Show, as both sides were busy practising. It was a fine day, and they practised racing on the track. They decided to abandon the tests they had planned, and instead drew up a race-card, to be run a few days after the Show. This was very exciting, and they each wrote out a copy, leaving spaces to write down the entries. Peter said that there should not be more than four in each race, as the course was too narrow. There were four flat races, and four races over jumps, which were called steeplechases, but were more like hurdle races.

Each pony was entered for two of each kind of race, and the ponies were classed and handicapped.

" Well," said Peter, " they are handicapped already, I suppose, by the rider's weight. We'd better keep to that, and not try to add weight."

" All right," agreed Ann, " but we could give Bess a few yards' start, you know. She is shorter than Silver and the other two." " The other two " were Sandy and Biscuits.

Jill and Peter had decided not to tell the Moors about training Prince, and were secretly wondering whether he could run in the races after the Show.

·   ·   ·   ·   ·   ·   ·   ·   ·

Jill's parents had done a lot of house-hunting, and seen a good many houses, and at last decided that one of them was suitable.

It was about three miles beyond the station, in all about seven miles away from the Hevers by road, but much less if you rode straight over the moor.

It lay on the outskirts of a small village, and had a large garden, and also several paddocks.

" Ah," said Mr. Crewe jokingly, " I shall settle down here and breed horses, I can see." Though he spoke lightly, he meant what he said, as he was very fond of, and interested in, horses.

The house itself was not large, but was comfortable and strongly built. It had an air of originality, and also a greatly approved large attic.

Jane had finished painting Bess, and Silver too. She had begun on the horses, and was considering the possibilities of a family group, with Nag, Nagina, and Prince.

This was more difficult, as it meant full or three-quarter views of the animals.

. . . .

But to return to Jill and Prince, the colt's training continued rapidly but steadily, and under more difficulty, for now the grown-ups were about more, and Peter had to set a watch at times, in case they should come back too soon, or go out for an unexpected walk. Peter was so careful, however, that they were never caught, although they several times came near it. Meanwhile Pat continued to feed Prince a few oats each day, which made all the difference to his work.

He was fresh each morning, but not enough to get out of control, just enough to make him stand up to the hard and continuous training.

The fourth day of his jumping, he was made to jump stiles, gates and parallel bars, all forms of plain bars. He took to these quite well, and in the afternoon Jill tried him over a red-and-white bar, of which he was suspicious, but at last accepted. Peter then set up a hog's back, as a preparation for the triple bar.

Jill walked him round it once or twice, so that he knew what it was like, and then set him at it. He rose unusually far away, and put a lot of length into the spring. Jill was not expecting it to last so long, and became rather unbalanced.

Prince objected to the uneven weight on his back, and started to buck. Jill could not soothe him down, he only got worse, and in the end she came off. Before Peter could run over to her, however, Prince had stopped bucking and trotted over to her, and was sniffing her hand.

" You all right?" asked Peter.

" Hm," said Jill doubtfully, " I've bashed this knee a

PRINCE MAKES FRIENDS AGAIN

bit. No, it's okay," she went on, standing up. She mounted Prince again and made him take the jump. This time she was prepared, and nothing unusual happened.

"Gosh!" exclaimed Peter afterwards, as they were putting Prince in his box, " he must like you, to stop like that and come over to see what's wrong. You have got a sort of spell over him."

"Oh, surely not," Jill laughed. They shut the loose-box door, and went to clean the tack.

"You know what," said Peter, " someone'll guess we've used this tack, soon. Lucky it isn't long to the Show now. It's getting much more dangerous."

"I heard Mrs. Hever say they'd found a prospective buyer for Prince last night."

"Gosh! did you? Well, she mustn't say anything defi-nite yet."

"I don't suppose she will, before the Show. Now that Mum and Dad have found a house, they'll be around the place more than ever."

"Oh, well, we'll manage somehow."

. . . .

The next day Prince was introduced to the wall-jump. He took a long time to get used to it, and at first refused even to look at it. After much persuasion he looked it well over, and then Peter told Jill to jump a row of wooden bricks on the ground first, as the box wouldn't go lower than 2 ft. 6 in.

Eventually Prince got used to it, and could jump up to 3 ft. 6 in. over it, which Peter said was enough.

On the sixth day, which was the 4th Sept., they made him jump the plain bar at 4 ft. 6 in. so that he should have something in hand on the day of the Show. By now his style of jumping was much better, having been formed by serious, hard jumping, which he seemed to enjoy. It was easy to see that he was Nag's son, for he had the same extra lift in his body, and the same light landing, which flowed smoothly into a collected stride again.

The same day he jumped a brush with a ditch, or rather a brush with a white bar laid in front of it about 3 ft. away. He also practised the Hog's Back several times.

It was amazing for Jill to realize how much the colt had progressed in about a week. His hind-quarters had much more power in them, or rather he had learnt to use their power to the best advantage, and all his movements were much more collected and graceful, although he had been graceful enough before. Jill did not realize, of course, how much she herself had progressed.

The day after that Prince was introducecd to the triple bar, which he accepted indifferently. After much practice he jumped it well, but soon he refused to jump another obstacle. He had been rushed through his training, and was tired of all this novelty and hard work. Jill persuaded him and kicked him lightly, but still he refused to jump, so she cantered him once round the field, and then Peter said:

" Make him try a very low 3 ft. bar, and then we'll stop He must jump just one more." So Jill cantered him at the jump. He refused again, and after much persuasion stepped over the jump. Jill left it at that, and gave him some practice at circling before going for a short ride into the other fields with Peter. Prince enjoyed the freedom and wanted to gallop, so Jill let him. His stride and action had improved, and he had far more spring. Peter noted his fine action, and thought of the speed he would probably have later on.

" I say, Jill," Peter called, kicking Bracken to make

him keep up, " you'll be able—oh, I say, pull him in a bit, I can't keep up—I was just saying that you'll be able to enter him for our races."

" Gosh! do you think so?" panted Jill, pulling Prince from a gallop to a canter, to a trot, and finally to a walk. " But what about Freddy?"

" Oh, John can ride him as well. That means he'll ride in every race. Still, he's going to be a jockey, after all."

" By the way, has Pat told her mother?" Jill and Peter turned homewards.

" Yes, and she doesn't object in moderation. She says that one day's racing won't hurt as long as we don't flog the ponies too hard. We've asked her to come up, you know."

" Is she going to?" asked Jill.

" Yes, all four grown-ups are," said Peter. " Look, Jill, after this ride we'd better rest Prince for to-day. He's physically and mentally tired."

" All right," said Jill, leaning forward to pat Prince. The rest of the morning Jill and Peter spent in Prince's box, sitting on the two mangers and chatting quietly about the Show. Every now and again Prince would come up to Jill or Peter, usually Jill, and demand some attention, either a pat or a carrot.

Peter forbade him to have sugar now, in case he should have too much, and get out of condition. That morning he was telling Jill about the points to remember in show-jumping. He suddenly remembered and promised that Prince should have some practice with the others standing round the outside of the jumps, making the usual atrocious noises and actions that the spectators usually do at Shows.

That afternoon the children rode over to see the new house, with the grown-ups. Mrs. Hever could not ride fast yet, as her arm was still stiff, though out of plaster, and so the party was rather slow. It was some time since Mrs. Crewe had ridden, so she appreciated the slow pace. She was riding Sandra, who was quite quiet, her husband Ben, Mrs. Hever Nag, and Mr. Hever Nagina.

Mrs. Hever insisted on riding in the Show, and her husband gave in. She was so excited at that unexpected prospect, that she talked all the way of their entries and hopes.

The children were very interested to look over the house, and even more the garden. Jill chose a room which she wanted, and then all the children dashed up to explore the attic. After a picnic tea they ran round the garden and thoroughly explored it, and then it was time to go home again.

. . . .

When, two days later, Jill woke up, she realized that it was the 7th, that Tim was coming and that Prince must do his very best. The rain was spattering against the windows, and after breakfast it began to pour. Jill felt very nervous.

" Don't worry!" Peter whispered to her as they cleared breakfast. " He went very well on those rounds yesterday. He's had a lot of practice, you know, and improved a good deal."

" Yes," said Jill, " but he still knocks the box each time."

" Yes, it *is* his worst jump, but don't worry! There's two days yet."

Tim turned up in the afternoon, and met Peter in the barn, as they had arranged.

" Gosh!" exclaimed Peter, " you came on a motor bike!"

" Yes," replied the little man, " it's the only means of

fast transport. I borrowed it from my brother. I don't hold with the things myself," he grinned.

Soon afterwards Mrs. Hever drove the Crewes over to the new house, to see about decorating and repairs. Mr. Hever was over the other side of his fields, seeing about the sheep which were to go to market. They were penned up there, and he had some job to do that he said would take about two days, so Peter thought it was safe to bring Prince out. The rain had slackened, and the sky showed little patches of blue.

Jill saddled Prince with trembling fingers, and looked into the pony's eyes before taking him out. She brushed his forelock out of his eyes, and said:

" Now, Prince, it's very important what you do now. You must do your best."

Prince pushed his nose into her pocket for a carrot. " No!" she murmured, and led him out. She mounted and rode down to the field. Tim gasped as he saw the colt.

" Well, isn't he lovely!" he exclaimed.

Jill cantered once round the field, glancing at the round of jumps Tim had put up. There was a triple bar in the middle, to be taken last, about 3 ft. at the highest bar, and four other jumps, one an in-and-out, one a wall, one a brush and the other a gate.

She set Prince at the first and he sailed over, also the second. The next was the wall, out of which Prince knocked two bricks, and then he cleared the third rather awkwardly, and swung round sharply into the triple bar, which presented little difficulty.

Tim was obviously all admiration, though he said little. After watching a few different rounds, in which he offered bits of advice, he had to go, and, leaving a list of things to notice and practise, he wished them luck.

CHAPTER XIX

Prince Wins

The morning of the Horse Show came at last. It was fine, with a beautiful sky of delicate blue, and a light mist on the trees. Jill woke early, and went down to give Prince a good grooming.

She worked hard for about half an hour on the colt, who stood waiting patiently for her to finish. He liked the touch of her hand as she wiped his face with a cloth, and he did not mind his delicate skin being tickled with the dandy-brush when she was brushing him.

When she had finished, his coat glowed and rippled in the dull light of the stables, his tail hung in a soft curve, each hair separate, and his mane curled softly over the ridge of his neck, the right side of which was caressed gently by the length of hair.

Jill anxiously felt his legs. They were firm and cool, and she sighed with relief. The day before Prince had been made to practise Tim's hints over and over again, until he could do two perfect rounds of jumps in successsion. Unfortunately, in the evening his legs had become rather hot, and Pat had warned Jill that he might not be fit enough to jump.

In consequence, Jill had spent a somewhat sleepless night, and had been glad to feel his sound legs while she had brushed them.

Soon after she had finished him, the other children

came down and began to groom their ponies, which had been
brought into stables the evening before. Jill therefore had
to turn to and groom Freddy, and by the time she had
really done her duty by him, she felt extremely tired.

While they were grooming the ponies Mr. Hever came
down, followed by Mr. Crewe, to begin grooming the
horses. When Peter and Pat had finished, they went to
help the two men, as there were six horses to do, and the
other three children went round to give out a little hay to
each horse, and to fill all the water-buckets.

There was some way to go to the Horse Show, which
was on the road beyond the station. Mr. Hever did not
want to short-cut over the moor on the horses, and reckoned
on taking two and a half hours to get there. The ponies
would take less time, possibly only two hours.

So half an hour after breakfast at 8.0, the grown-ups
mounted and set off.

This was lucky, for the children could see Prince into
Tim's horse-box. He arrived at about ten to nine, and
Jill led Prince into the second compartment of the box,
and haltered him to the ring on the wall. She threw the
saddle and bridle in front of him.

" Better rug him up," said Tim, " in case anyone looks
inside. They might recognize him so easily."

Jill fetched a linen rug, and girthed it loosely round
the colt.

.   .   .   .

Two hours later they arrived at the Show, and having
tied the ponies up near the other horses, they went to get
their numbers to tie on their arms. Mr. and Mrs. Crewe
were not riding, and had secured good seats at the ringside on two stools. The children went and stood by them
in the first event, for Heavy Hunters.

Ben and Sandra were entered, with Mr. and Mrs. Hever as their respective riders. Ben was liked by the judges, and won third prize, but Sandra was not really in the same class.

In the Best Hack class, both the Arabs were entered, and the judges could hardly avoid awarding them the first two prizes. Nag was first.

John was entered in the next class, for the smaller ponies, and the others wished him luck as he went off to get Bess. He had no luck, unfortunately, although he was called into the first row, with only eight others, which showed that Bess was being considered.

As that class cantered out, the other four ran over to mount their ponies for the next class, for the bigger ponies. Jill felt nervous, and she and Jane grinned at each other as they waited to enter the ring, for both were new to riding in shows.

It seemed easier, however, as soon as they were inside the ropes, and the time passed like a dream for the two girls. All four ponies were considered in the first row, and the judges found it hard to decide between Bracken and Sunny. They asked the ages of the two, and on finding that Sunny was only four, they gave him 2nd prize and Bracken 3rd.

Jill and Jane were secretly sorry that their two had been ignored, but were proud to be in the first row, and glad that their friends had won. The 1st prize-winner was a very fine grey mare with dark markings.

After that exertion the children were glad to join John at the ringside to watch the Light Hunter class. Firefly and Doricles were in for this, again ridden by Mr. and Mrs. Hever. The two horses were both placed, being very fine compact animals, good at jumping. Doricles was 3rd and Firefly reserve.

The class after that was Driving, and they had nothing entered. Everyone sat down and had some lemonade while they watched.

" It's the lunch interval after the two riding classes," said Mr. Hever.

John was in the next class, for riders under 12, and he proved his worth by winning 1st prize.

" Good old John!" the others called as they passed him. He was cantering out of the ring, and they into it, for their Riding Class.

" Oh, I'm nervous!" Jill whispered to Pat.

" Oh, don't worry," said Pat kindly. " It'll be better when you're in there."

Jill felt glad she had been in the other class. It would have been terrible to start off with a riding class.

She called to mind all the advice her host and hostess had given her, and tried to look natural as well.

It was soon over, with Peter winning second prize. Jill almost won reserve, but the judge decided in favour of a boy with fine hands.

" Bad luck!" whispered Jane.

In a few minutes they were out of the ring again, and tying up the ponies. They led them over to a water-tank, after removing their saddles, and then gave them some hay.

Then they all sat down to a very welcome lunch. Welcome, that is, to all except Jill, whose stomach was turning over and doing jigs, as far as she could feel. Prince was either to be covered with glory or seriously condemned in the second class after lunch! Novice Jumping came just after Open Jumping, which was to start off the afternoon.

Mr. Hever was riding Ben and Nagina in Open Jumping, and Mrs. Hever just Nag.

" Oh, well," Mr. Hever told his wife jokingly, but

meaning what he said, " you'll get first, anyway, so Nag's worth two horses any day."

He was right. Nag and Nagina and two other horses got a clear round the first time. Ben got two faults, through knocking the triple bar, and equalled two other horses. In the jump-off, Nag again got a clear round, but the others all made some mistakes on the slightly higher jumps. Ben beat the other horses with two faults in a jump-out, and therefore got reserve. Nag was 1st and Nagina 3rd.

During this class Peter and Pat and Jill had been over by Tim's horse-box. Firefly and Freddy were with them, so that as soon as this class were over, they could go straight to the collecting ring. Jill was suffering terribly from " butterflies in the stomach " and would have given anything not to have entered at all.

Tim had actually entered Prince for the class in the lunch interval, to avoid any suspicion on the part of the steward, who knew of Prince as owned by the Hevers, but thought it was a different animal when entered by Tim.

At last the time came when Jill had to take the colt to the collecting ring. Luckily the crowds were so thick round the ring that the four grown-ups and Jane and John could not see Jill over on the other side. She had to keep Prince slightly apart from the other ponies, for he was nervous and restless with the new sights, sounds and smells.

Peter and Pat were sitting on their animals near her, and even the hardy Peter looked a little anxious. He looked at Jill.

" Good luck !" he said. After a silence he added : " Gosh, I hope you get him round all right ! Think what the Hevers will feel like when they see you ! Oh, gosh !" He shivered.

" Shall we go through with it ?"

" Why, of course!" Pat chimed in encouragingly. Several people came up to admire Prince, and Jill began to feel a little better. She studied the jumps, and saw that they were not too difficult.

" Come along now!" shouted the steward; " someone start it off."

A girl on a chestnut gelding was pushed into the ring. She circled once, and started off. There were seven jumps. She made several faults, and cantered out with a grim expression. Several people tried the jumps after her. One girl on a grey got a clear round. Then Pat was urged into the ring by the hot and bothered steward. She did a steady, well-judged round on Freddy, and made no mistakes.

" Come along," said the steward, suddenly seeing Jill. " I'll bet that black can jump well. You go next."

Jill's nerves stormed for a minute, then everything seemed to snap, and she found that she felt quite calm and had lost all fear, as if she were numb.

She clicked her tongue to encourage Prince, and he leapt forward into the ring, sensing and taking on her new courage and determination. She circled him once, and then steadied him for the first jump. For a moment she thought he was going to refuse the ordinary bar, but he sprang quite slowly, and took the jump unhurriedly.

And that was how he completed the round. He cantered round the ring slowly and collectedly, almost taking the jumps in his stride. Where Jill had been filled with fear and anxiety, there was now a sense of astonishing security and wondering admiration. She hardly had to move on the pony, as they cleared brush, gate, box and parallel bars with perfect ease. Next came the in-and-out, which Prince dealt with nimbly, and he sailed over the triple bar in one marvellous spring.

After a few moments' pause, the spectators applauded the round loudly. Jill suddenly realized that their object was achieved, and that there was nothing more to be anxious about. She could not speak as she cantered out of the ring and up to Peter and Pat. They, too, said nothing for a minute, but patted her on the back.

" Gosh !" Peter gulped. " You were both marvellous. That triple bar !"

" Oh, Jill," sighed Pat, " you *are* lucky, being able to ride him so well! I bet Mum and Dad are pleased !"

Peter was called off next, and also did a clear round on the very tricky and fiery Firefly. There were six clear rounds to jump out after everyone had gone round, Jill, Peter, Pat, the girl on the grey, a boy on a beautiful chestnut, and another girl on a short and sturdy bay.

The jumps were raised a little, and Peter had to go round first. He dealt firmly with Firefly, who was feeling playful, and managed to get a clear round. Then the bay went in and made two faults. The girl rode the grey in and, with almost a clear round, just tipped the box and knocked the slat off. The chestnut got a clear round with ease, and then Pat went in.

Jill watched anxiously, patting Prince's neck. Freddy jumped superbly, although the jumps were a little too high for him, and he had to make an effort. He got a clear round again.

Then Jill had to take Prince round once more. He was not tired, however, and although the jumps were higher, he made another clear round. Jill noticed that the box, his worst jump still, had not been altered, but it had to have another layer of bricks for the final jump-out, when the jumps were again raised a little.

The chestnut went round first, and got a clear round.

Then Peter went, and made two faults, for Firefly was getting extremely excited and careless. Jill went next. Prince began to put more effort into his jumping, and Jill had to urge him forward to each jump. He cleared them all, however, until they got to the box. Here he was tired, and dropped a hind leg in mid-air, knocking off the slat. He landed badly, and Jill stopped him completely for a minute before finishing the course without a mistake, which put him second behind the chestnut.

Pat then went round on the brave little Freddy, but the jumps were too high for him, and he made about twelve faults, therefore getting reserve.

As soon as the three children cantered out of the ring after the boy on the chestnut, who was first, they were besieged by the other two and the grown-ups.

" Jill, how marvellous !" Mrs. Hever exclaimed.

" Oh, Jill," her father said, " you shouldn't have done it, you know."

" Yes, dear," her mother agreed, " it was wrong to do it without Mr. Hever's permission."

" Oh, never mind that !" cried that excited man. " She's done it ! That's all that matters. We never even guessed. And none of the horses entered even got a clear round ! Those shorter ones always do better."

CHAPTER XX

The Final Decision

After all that excitement, the rest of the Show seemed rather dull. John went in for children's jumping under 12 and made four faults. He was about 8th, but of course did not win a prize. Then came the jumping class for the other children. Freddy was still quite tired, but the jumps were much lower than in the Novice, and Jill got a clear round on him. Silver played up, and got disqualified at the box for refusing three times.

Bracken and Sunny also made clear rounds, with Ann on Berry, who had only just arrived at the Show with her brothers.

" Sandy cast a shoe," she explained hastily to Peter as they met in the collecting ring, " so we had to go and get another put on, which took time."

In the jump-out, Ann got a first, Peter second, another girl on a brown third, and Pat reserve. Jill made many mistakes on the tired Freddy.

Then came the Touch and Out class for jumping. It was Open, and had attracted a good entry. Nag, Ben, Nagina and Doricles were in for this. After two rounds of jumping, very few were left in with no mistakes. Nag and Nagina were still in the running. The entries were gradually thinned down to five, and then to three. Nagina went out next, and Nag had to fight it out with a splendidly-built grey hunter.

Newcomers to the district were surprised to see a stallion competing for a jumping class, but most of the people there knew Nag, and were not surprised at the good manners of the strong and fiery animal, when Mrs. Hever was riding him.

In the end he triumphed, when the bar stood at 5 ft. 6 in. and the triple bar at 5 ft. Jill began to understand the power and grace latent in Prince, and the beautiful romance of heredity occurred to her. Peter and she caught each other's eyes, and each saw that the other's were filled with the pride and joy of achievement.

" They're having a short break now!" called Mr. Hever, riding up on Nagina. " Come and help take off the saddles, and then we'll have tea!"

During tea Jill was plied with a rapid cross-fire of questions, which she answered rather shortly, still feeling too full of emotion to talk much. The one thing she did wax fluent about was Peter's part in the training, which she praised inordinately, to cover her confusion partly at all the praise heaped on her.

" Oh no," said Peter modestly, " you've been the real working-part."

" Well," said Jane laughingly, " as they're both so modest, let's say that Prince is the real hero!"

" Hear, hear!" shouted everyone, laughingly serious. The people near them looked round in curiosity, but they did not care.

" Come on, Jill," said Mrs. Hever, " eat up! You hardly had any lunch, and you must be hungry now!"

" Oh no, thanks awfully," Jill grinned. " At lunch I was terribly nervous and felt sick, and now I still feel sick, but just from joy and excitement, and—and I don't know what."

Everyone laughed and patted her on the back.

. . . .

As for the gymkhana classes, John was in the Musical Chairs, and got third prize. In the Open Bending, Firefly and Sandra competed against all the ponies except John's little Bess, and it was very exciting. Firefly, with Mrs. Hever, won the Bending, and Freddy actually got reserve, which was good in the fierce competition of skilful animals.

In the last class Peter got a second, and Jane reserve, as both Bracken and Silver were fast and handy, and ideal for Obstacle races.

After all that excitement and all those heat-making exertions, everyone finished up the lemonade, including Tim, Ann, and her brothers. Mr. Hever had a long technical and extremely horsey argument with Tim, while the others discussed the happenings of the day, and worked out their total winnings.

" Well," said Mrs. Hever, getting up, " it's time we started for home."

" Oh yes," said Tim, " I must get back with the horses."

" You got a first in the hunter, didn't you?" asked Peter.

" Yes, with Jack in the Box. And a third in Open Jumping with Bluebird."

" Oh yes! Of course. He's a beauty."

" By the way, Peter, my boy," Tim went on, " you can come over and ride on exercise at our stables if you like. I know you're keen on training and racing, and it would be a bit of experience."

" Lucky chap, Peter," said Mr. Hever.

" Gosh, thanks, Tim!" Peter agreed.

" I'm sorry not to be able to take John too," said Tim

kindly, "but I'm afraid he's a little too small. And I'd take you girls as well, if I didn't know that the trainer has a prejudice against women-riders," he added tactfully.

Jill's parents had been rather silent up to now, feeling indeed quite in awe of their daughter, who had changed a lot, and seemed to have developed in a way that filled them with astonishment.

After the long ride home, however, and then having to unsaddle Freddy and Prince, Jill was so tired that she leaned against her father's shoulder as they went into the house, and then flopped down beside her mother on the sofa, and was soon asleep with her head on the loving shoulder.

As soon as Jill needed care and help, her parents realized that in most ways she was just the same as ever, and were now ready to bustle about and carry her up to bed and get her hot drinks, and so on. The others were almost as tired, and soon went up to bed too.

The four parents sat round the fire, and tried to see into the future.

.   .   .   .

The next morning, at breakfast, everyone was discussing Prince.

"I think we shall have to see you ride him again," Mrs. Hever was saying.

"I don't know how you trained him to jump like that in about a month. When did you start training him?" asked Mr. Hever, his grey eyes serious.

"Oh, about a month ago," said Peter, "but he's only been jumping for just under two weeks. I never thought we'd get him ready for the Show."

"Good Heavens!" exclaimed Mr. Hever; "but why did you have to enter him for that? I mean, it might not have worked out."

"No, I know," said Pat, taking up the cause, "but you said that you wanted to sell him, and we wanted to show you once and for all that Jill can manage him perfectly."

"But why Jill in the first place, anyway?" asked Mr. Crewe. "He's going to be your horse, isn't he?"

"Oh yes, he was, but Jill's much better with him. Actually, of course, it was Jill's and Peter's idea at first. I didn't know till a bit later."

"We got the idea when I noticed how quiet Prince was with Jill," Peter explained.

"Oh, I see," said Jill's mother.

"Well, anyway, I should go and get Prince ready, and we'll come down in a minute or two," Mrs. Hever said.

The children hurried out into the crisp autumn air, and discovered a light frost on the grass.

"Gosh," said Pat delightedly, "the first we've had! I shall be hunting Sunny soon." And they ran down to the stables with light hearts.

Back in the dining-room, the grown-ups were discussing Prince.

"Well," Mr. Hever was just saying, "if you want to get Jill a pony, you couldn't do better than Prince. She can manage him all right."

"But what about Pat?" asked Mrs. Crewe. "She does seem very fond of the pony, and after all, Jill didn't tell her."

"Well, if you're at all doubtful," Mrs. Hever broke in, "let Pat try to ride Prince. We'll see who Prince likes best."

"I suppose you're right," said Mr. Crewe doubtfully.

"That is the fairest way. Let's clear this stuff into the kitchen, and then go down."

So five minutes later everyone stood in the field, leaning against the fence, and watching Jill circle Prince outside the jumps, at a walk, trot and canter as ordered by Peter, who was standing in the middle of the circle.

Then he called her into the circle, and told her to back, passage and trot in a figure of eight. After that Prince had to do a low brush jump.

"Jolly good!" called Mr. Hever.

And then Jill provided the opportunity the grown-ups had been waiting for.

"Would you like to try him?" she asked Pat. "You mustn't give him up too easily."

"Gosh, thanks!" said Pat eagerly.

Jill dismounted, and held Prince's head while Pat got up. Then Pat urged him forward. He obeyed unwillingly, though, as Jill had told him to, he trotted and cantered all right, but he absolutely refused to jump, despite all Pat's urgings and pleadings, and when she dug her heels into his sides, he put his head down and bucked just once. Pat stayed on, but his decision was obvious.

The grown-ups thanked the children for showing them Prince, and went off again, without telling Jill anything definite about Prince's ownership.

All the children felt that there was something in the air, and it made them restless.

"Gosh," sighed Jane, "it's ages since we went to the hideout! Let's go up this afternoon."

"Ooh, yes!" shrieked John, hopping energetically on one foot.

"I suppose I'd better not ride Prince," said Jill; "he had enough exercise yesterday."

"Yes," Peter agreed, "I should give him a rest. Of course, Freddy's pretty tired."

"I don't suppose he is now," said Pat, "he always picks up again quickly."

So early after lunch they packed up tea and sandwiches, and trotted down the road to the woods.

.   .   .   .

They found Ann and the twins at the hideout too, and went for a ride down the stream with them. The country was not very different, however, and they soon returned, to sit on the ground outside the hut and watch their ponies grazing. They talked about many things.

"When do your holidays end?" John asked suddenly. "We go back on the 22nd."

"Oh, we don't go till the 25th," Jack boasted, "but it takes a day to get there. It's in Yorkshire."

"That's funny, mine's in Yorkshire too," cried Jill. "We go back on the 23rd."

"Oh, we have to go back on the 18th," Pat groaned. "Or was it changed, Jane?"

"No, I'm afraid not," sighed Jane. "I say, Jill, couldn't you come to our school? It'd be ever such fun having you with us. It's in Dorset, quite near the sea."

"Well, I'll ask Dad," said Jill. "It would be fun. When do you go, Ann?"

"Not till the 28th. I'm jolly pleased, except that Bill and Jack won't be here after the 25th. Still, there'll be time to hunt a bit. But let's get on to a pleasanter subject," she went on. "What are we racing in on Saturday? Of course, now you've got that smashing Arab, it'll be a walk-over."

"Hardly," said Peter, "at least not in the jumping, 'cos he's only just learnt."

" I don't believe it!" exclaimed Ann. " Why, he jumps like a professional!"

" Well he is," Jill insisted.

" Oh, by the way, Pat," said Peter, " do you mind if John rides Freddy as well as Bess? He is going to be a jockey, and he can enter all the races then." Pat nodded, and smiled at John.

Then they went on discussing the races while they had tea.

. . . .

That evening the children trotted into the yard, and turned their ponies out into the field. The grown-ups were in the garden, and the children went over and sat down near them.

" Jill," said Mrs. Hever suddenly, " we've decided that Prince is going to be your pony. Your father's bought him, and he's now your own."

" Oh, gosh!" said Jill, her eyes sparkling. " Oh, gosh, thanks awfully! But what about Pat? I mean, she likes him too, and he's really hers."

" Oh no, Jill," said Pat rather quietly, " you can look after him better. After all, you deserve him with all the work you've put into his training." She was feeling the wrench badly, and couldn't bear the thought that Prince was actually Jill's, but she bravely kept to her word, and to what she knew was right.

For a moment Jill realized how she was feeling, but then her own joy overcame all other emotions, and she ran down to the stables to see Prince.

She went into his box, and with her hands round the top of his neck and her face pressed against his nose, she whispered to him, crying in her joy. He stood quiet, waiting

JILL'S OWN PONY!

for her to finish. Soon she stood back once more, and wiped her eyes and blew her nose, still feeling rather tearful.

"Oh, Prince," she laughed through her tears, her eyes smarting with salt, "I am a fool, aren't I? But you don't mind."

Then she put on his saddle and bridle, and was just leading him out into the yard when Peter ran up.

"Going for a ride?" he shouted. "Let me come too, and we can race Prince and Bracken. Not too much, of course, or he'll get tired. Gosh, you are lucky! I'll get Bracken's tack."

So Jill and Peter had a short gallop along by the river. Prince naturally won their race, not having gone for a long, tiring ride in the afternoon. The sun was getting lower, but the air had not the keen nip of the early morning, and the two friends walked their ponies back slowly, saying little, but happy that everything had gone right.

When they returned, they found the others still with the grown-ups in the garden. They turned Prince and Bracken out in the field, and now sat down on the grass and rested.

"Oh, by the way, Dad," Jill said lazily, "do you think I could go to Pat's school? Jane's there as well, and I'd love to be at the same one. It's in Dorset too."

"Well, I'll see, dear," answered her father, looking at his wife.

"Oh, good," sighed Jill.

"I say, Jill," Jane piped up, "shall I start Prince's portrait now? I'll do one of you on his back, if you like."

"Oh no," said Jill. "Better unsaddled."

The five children wandered down to the field, Jane with a sketching book in her hand. Suddenly, as she talked to

Jill, Pat realized that her friendship mattered more to her than Prince, and was glad she had let him go to Jill.

And Jill? Why, she was perfectly contented, as she stood behind Jane's shoulder, in the midst of her friends, and watched the growing likeness of Prince appearing on Jane's paper, the likeness of that beautiful, glowing colt who stood before them, curiously watching.